TOUGH GIRLS
Don't Dance

Osmund
JAMES

Cover Design by: Sanya Dockery
Typeset by: Janet Campbell

Published by: LMH Publishing Limited
7 Norman Road
LOJ Industrial Complex
Building 10 -11
Kingston C.S.O., Jamaica
Tel: 876-938-0005; 938-0712
Fax: 876-759-8752
Email: lmhbookpublishing@cwjamaica.com
Website: www.lmhpublishing.com

Printed in U.S.A.   ISBN: 978-976-8184-08-5

Tough Girls
Don't Dance

Prologue

It is said that women born in the zodiac sign Taurus (the bull) are usually more aggressive than the most aggressive men. The Taurus woman doesn't forgive easily, especially those whom she had originally loved. And she will go to great lengths to gain vengeance against her adversaries.

My life up to now has been a testament of these sayings about us Taurus women.

But over the past four months, and for the first time since I was nine years old, I have found true happiness. When I was fourteen I vowed never to marry nor have children. But now I am a mature woman, three months pregnant who has a wonderful husband whom I adore.

Up until my marriage, my life was a series of bitter experiences, many of which I am now ashamed of and have been trying to forget since I got married four months ago. My husband knows about a few of these blots on my past. I decided to tell him about my other shameful memories, and he said I should write them down as if I was writing a novel. Can't say why, but I feel compelled to share every detail of my shockingly sordid past with my husband; a past more lustful and dirty than you could imagine.

I know it is possible my husband will forsake me when he realizes just how immoral my past was. The thought of losing him makes me tremble with fear, but I must write it all down for him to read. And perhaps by writing it down I shall then be able to get rid of the shame which burdens me when my husband isn't at home.

It is surprising how clear each event of my past is in my mind, as if I am living it all over again...God knows I wouldn't want to...once was enough...more than enough.

C.C.

Chapter 1

"This is good for yu," my stepfather said in a soft coaxing voice. His large, coarse, brown hand was massaging my hairless crotch. I was nine years old and scared. I wanted to flee from his lap, but his strong hand held me firmly against his powerful and hairy chest.

I had been born in my maternal grandparents' three-room board house in Belfield, St Mary on the night of the 19th of May 1960 – my mother was then seventeen years old. The man she said was my father disowned me – never accepted me as his child – and his family ignored me, and he migrated to England when I was two years old. I was given my grandparents' (mother's) surname. Thus I was registered as Carlene Clark.

My grandparents were in their late fifties when I was born. I was their fifth grandchild, my mother's first born: Momma was the youngest of three children, all girls. My older aunt, who was ten years older than momma, and her husband and their three children lived about a mile from my grandparents. The younger aunt, who was seven years older than momma, was still living at home and had a boy two years older than me. I had grandaunts and granduncles and second cousins scattered all over the district, which is one of the larger rural districts in Jamaica.

My grandparents were from very poor origins, born, like most of the district's older heads, in thatched wattle and daub huts. But grandpa's parents had seen to it that he learned to read and write; which was why he had been able to rise to the position of headman on one of the nearby properties. Grandma, who couldn't read and write much, was one of those women who could do as much farm work as any man. Her two-acre farm behind the house was always clean and well forked. They were 'moderate' Anglicans but their three children grew up to be unattached to any church.

When I was four years old my mother and I went to live with her lover, Mr Harry. He lived about ten chains above my grand-

parents' home on the narrow unpaved lane called Grasspiece Gully
– the lane was steep where it began on the main road, then lev-
elled off after about twenty chains and ended up on the bank of a
river; all told the lane was about half a mile long. Mr Harry was ten
years older than momma, and, like momma and myself, he had a
medium-brown complexion. He had a small farm and also worked
on one of the large estates which surrounded our hilly district. His
hair was always trimmed low and face clean-shaven.

He wasn't a native of Belfield, but had moved there from
Portland when I was one year old. Two of his distant cousins were
already living in Belfield when he moved there. He didn't arrive
in Belfield penniless; as soon as he came he bought his small farm
and built a two-bedroom board house – by the time momma and
I went to live with him he had added another room and a small
verandah. He was pleasant looking, muscular and of medium
height, and had charmed me from the beginning with his interesting stories and by calling me his 'first born'.

But I was to find out that he was an evil man, who had had to
sell his inheritance and flee from the wrath of his neighbours in
Portland.

Belfield is a farming district set amongst the low hills that overlook the narrow coastal plain in eastern St Mary – northeastern
Jamaica. The hills are wide with steep slopes and deep gullies that
run off into the two rivers which flank the three-mile long district.
The main road runs up the middle and lanes branch off at regular
intervals, usually going downhill. The main crops are bananas
and cocoa. From most points the sea can be seen less than seven
miles away.

I don't remember much of life before my seventh birthday, but
I do have vague memories about my grandfather's death when I
was five and grandma's death – due to a broken heart everyone
said – a year later. I seem to recall that there had been a slight driz-
zle at both funerals and that I didn't cry until after everything was
over.

After my grandparents' deaths the father of my younger

4

aunt's two children went to live with her, at what I was always to think of as my grandfather's house. Momma gave birth to Mr Harry's first child, a son, four months after grandma's death.

Our lane was still then not really much more than a foot-track – in 1971 it was widened by the parish council but left unpaved until 1975. I used to love when it rained so I could walk barefoot in the dark-brown mud with my cousins. Up to 1973 electricity was confined to the main road, and we had to carry water from the nearest spring or the stand-pipe on the main road – both spring and pipe were about a quater mile from my home; because the journey from the spring was uphill we used the pipe as long as water wasn't locked off. I was greatly relieved when they extended the water system down onto our lane in 1973 and Mr Harry immediately ran a pipe into our yard.

But by then I was a troubled teenager, though I had been very happy up to my twelfth birthday. Our district was poor but happy, with its close-knit families and abundant fruit trees. I especially used to love to go and collect wood for fuel on the nearest estate, which had many tracks of logwood trees thickly grown. As a pre-teen I went with momma and Mr Harry each Saturday afternoon, later on I would prefer to go with my cousins and school friends – boys and girls – in large groups.

Another sign of our district's poverty was the fact that up to 1977 ninety percent of the homes were small board houses with out-house toilets (usually of zinc) and bamboo kitchens. Our out-house was behind the house on the edge of Mr Harry's two-and-a-half acre cocoa and banana farm, which was on a gentle slope. Our airy bamboo kitchen was to the left of the house, which was slightly below the level of our lane. The house, three rooms and a verandah, had a zinc roof that was painted red, cream coloured sand-dashed outside walls and painted pale blue inside. There were only two houses within three chains of our home.

By the time momma and Mr Harry got married shortly after my eighth birthday I was calling him daddy and truly felt that I was his first child. I was a slightly plump child and everyone agreed that I

would grow up to be a raving beauty. I remember crying because momma and my step-daddy said I couldn't accompany them on their night out on the beach on the night of their wedding – they spent the night under a tree on a secluded beach. (How romantic, I thought!)

My dark memories began on a Saturday when I was nine; momma was then pregnant with her third child.

On Saturday mornings after breakfast momma went to buy groceries at a shop that was about a quarter of a mile away. My older aunt, who was a week-end higgler in Kingston, bought vegetables and seasonings for us in Kingston. Momma usually took me along to the shop on Saturday mornings, but on this Saturday in question she decided to leave me and my three-year-old brother Errol at home with daddy, who had announced that he was too tired to go to work on his farm that morning.

"Too much rum last night," momma teased, her eyes bright with that glow often seen on women in the early stages of pregnancy; she was then about ten weeks pregnant, but her belly was already prominent. And she was one of those women whom pregnancy made happy, brisk and super-strong.

"Yu know I wasn't even well tipsy when I come in last night," daddy said. "Plus I can hold my liquor an' know when to stop."

When momma floated out of the yard I was rinsing the last of the dishes and pots that she had washed. It was a bright morning, a cooling breeze flowed from off the sea. I turned down the last pot on the bamboo drainage-board in the kitchen and went to join my brother and step-daddy in the house. They were in the room we called the 'hall' – furnished with a five-piece dining table set, one of those old-time-styled tall cabinets (three shelves for crockery, a cupboard and two drawers), what rural folks called a 'centre-table' (somewhat like a coffee table) with a vase of plastic flowers and sea shells sitting on crochet pieces, and two all-wood arm-chairs.

The 'hall' was a small room with cheap pictures hanging on the walls. Daddy and my brother were listening to our small transistor radio. "Errol if you want yu can go look for Barry," daddy said

6

as soon as I entered from the verandah which faced the east and was now bathed with sunshine.

Errol gladly went next door to visit his best friend. "Close the door," daddy said, "an' come here. I hav' something to tell yu."

I was sure he meant a new story. With a glad heart I closed the front door, but the room remained bright because the curtains at the windows were thin. I skipped up to daddy. He was sitting in one of the arm-chairs, and lifted me onto his knees. I always loved sitting in his lap when he was telling one of his stories. But now when I snugly settled in his lap he gave me a scare by crushing me to his broad chest and began to caress my upper thigh. (I was wearing a ruffled dress that I had out-grown.)

"Yu heavy fo' a nine-year-old," he said softly. My initial fright lessened. "An'," he added flatteringly, "yu will soon be a woman."

Even at that early age I was susceptible to flattery, and my greatest desire was to grow up quickly. So although I was confused by daddy's passionate embrace and caressing hand, I was no longer alarmed. After all, wasn't he my step-daddy? He didn't and would never mean me any harm.

"All the boys will soon start to ask yu fo' sex," he said with gaiety. My uneasiness began to grow stronger. "How much do you know about sex?"

I blushed deeply and continued to avoid his eyes, my hands glued to the arm-rests. Of course, I had a fairly good idea about sex – facts overheard from the older girls at school and classmates who had been lucky enough to see parents or other adults in the act, and like all country kids I had witnessed the various types of farm animals 'doing it'. Yes, you learnt about sex early in Belfield. But I was only nine, I thought, it would be many years before I would be ready for sex.

Like a spider, daddy's hand crept up the inside of my thighs, his other hand pinning me to his chest. I stiffened and closed my legs tightly. Fear gripped me and I tried unsuccessfully to force my way out of his lap. (Momma had told me not to let anyone touch my vagina.)

"Don't be afraid," daddy cooed. He pulled his hand from

between my thighs and began to massage my plump hairless pelvis. "A would never hurt yu. A love yu."

My pulse was racing wildly and I realized daddy was breathing heavier than usual. I wanted to flee but he was too strong for me, and for some unknown reason I didn't try to force away his hand on my pelvis.

"Don't be afraid," he coaxed. "Relax." Then he began to shower hot kisses on my neck and temples. And I felt one of his fingers force its way down to my hairless pussy, massaging my little clit through my thin panty.

I began to tremble, and that was when he said, "This good for yu." Then he captured my interest by adding, "This will mek' yu grow fast," (I so wanted to grow fast!) "mek' yu grow real fast and pretty. But yu mustn't allow anybody else to do it. Only me mus' do it."

Daddy's hand was now producing a sweet and new sensation that quickly spread outward in waves to the rest of my body. Ecstasy – my first taste of it. My fear and trembling subsided. Still, a small part of my mind kept telling me daddy was wrong. But how could something which gave this type of pleasure be wrong? I closed my eyes and pushed aside the voice of caution, relaxing in daddy's embrace and floating on the pleasure he was giving me. Pleasure that would make me grow, grow, grow real fast and pretty.

"That's right, my dove," he said sweetly, "relax an' enjoy." Two minutes later he stopped massaging and kissed my lips. I opened my eyes and for the first time I became aware of his iron-hard penis against my hip. I slowly squirmed towards his knees wondering, with the beginning of a new fear, if he would now ask for sex. I glanced at his cloudy eyes and, as if reading my thoughts he said, "Yu still too young fo' sex, but what a jus' do is good for yu."

I relaxed once more, and my love and trust in him grew. I should've known, I thought penitently, Daddy wouldn't ask me for sex.

"My little love," he added soothingly, "yu mus' not let anybody else touch yu. An' don't tell anyone that I touch yu now. It is our

little secret. If you momma find out she will be jealous an' beat yu." I glanced at his hairless face.

"She say," I said timidly, eyes downcast and hands together, "I mustn't let anybody...touch me up."

"Because she know them boys an' men out a street will hurt yu," daddy explained. He turned my face up to his, cupping my chin gently, and I reluctantly met his eyes. "But I won't hurt yu. Jus' don't tell her I touch yu."

"I won't tell," I whispered with downcast eyes.

He kissed my lips and killed all doubts by saying, "Remember that is not everything that good to eat, good to talk. " I recalled that this phrase – which meant that not every good thing should be made public – had been one of my grandmother's favourite sayings and was now momma's favourite.

"Yu mother," Daddy said with a scholarly air, "want me to love her more than everybody else. But is yu who is my number one love." (I loved the sound of that and smiled up at him.) "Plus because me is not yu blood father there is nothing wrong with us being lovers."

After that day daddy became kinder to me. But he wasn't able to give me my second lesson until three weeks later – by which time I was masturbating almost every night.

Chapter 2

Momma loved 'dead-yards' – a home where somebody had died and wasn't yet buried (the term, 'dead-yard', had its origin in the fact that before the early seventies, poor rural folk kept their dead at home on large blocks of ice – bought from the ice-trucks which then plied the country-side daily – or buried the body within thirty hours after death). Daddy, on the other hand, who wasn't much of a singer, was casual about this popular rural entertainment of singing, feasting and the famous 'Dinki-Mini' folk dance. What drew momma to dead-yards was the nightly singing of hymns and the gossip groups. She had a lovely tenor voice that was perfect for dead-yard singing. Her voice was in much demand at every 'set-up' (big feast on the night before burial) and 'nine-night' (the feast on the ninth night after death).

At about 7:15 on a fair and cool Monday evening momma and a few of our neighbours left for a dead-yard which was about half a mile away. Daddy stayed with my brother and me. All evening I had been eagerly awaiting momma's going, looking forward to daddy's kisses and caresses which would make me grow and grow real fast. (I was convinced daddy's claim that his caresses would make me grow extra fast and pretty was fact, a great knowledge). Did any of my friends, I wondered, know that the kisses and caresses of a grown man would add extra speed to their growth? In any case I couldn't tell them because to do so would be to let out this wonderful and pleasurable secret I shared with daddy. Plus, I wanted to grow faster than my friends, to be the tallest in my class.

Yes, I mused, it would be great to be taller than my classmates who were now taller than me.

Half an hour after momma's cheerful departure my brother was asleep in daddy's lap. We were in the sitting room silently listening to the radio and enjoying the cool sea breeze blowing through the open front windows and front door.

Daddy carried my brother to bed in the room we two children

Shortly, his licking and sucking and nibbling of my pussy brought me the earth-shaking glory of my first orgasm.

Thereafter, whenever the opportunity arose, daddy pleasured me with his hands and mouth, and taught me the art of sucking a man's penis. From the first I loved the taste of a man's juice and I believed daddy's claim that drinking his would make me grow even more than his kisses and caresses. And he taught me the art of passionate kissing.

I am now sure he had learned about oral sex from tourists to whom he use to sell fruits back in Portland. Up to the eighties rural folk in non-tourist areas such as Belfield frowned on oral sex.

I told nobody about my affair with daddy and I was sure nobody, least of all momma, suspected us. Throughout the years that we were lovers, it is very doubtful that anyone did suspect us. Daddy's shady past, of which I was to learn many years later, was unknown in Belfield and he seemed to all to be an upright man.

In the meantime the other aspects of my life rolled on in the manner of the other little girls my age in Belfield. There was the challenge of learning all the aspects of housework. Here again I was in love with housework because it seemed a sign of maturity and I was obsessed with my foremost dream of being the woman of my own grand home. I was such a willing pupil, moreso than most of my friends, that momma was always boasting about the house. And by the time I was twelve I could wash, cook and iron fairly well.

With pride I now remember the day shortly after my eleventh birthday when momma went to the nearest town and, missing the early afternoon bus, returned home at dusk to find that I had single-handedly prepared rice and beans with curried chicken. For a whole week she boasted about this to all and sundry.

Momma wasn't a church member and daddy distrusted all preachers and priests, so I rarely went to Sunday School. At that early age I found church boring, even the livelier Pentecostal Assemblies.

At school I was an average student academically and one of those shrewd pranksters who rarely ever was the source of a teacher's wrath -- the jokes and pranks were always timely and made the teachers laugh, and, most importantly, I wasn't a chatterbox. Rarely was I subject to the teachers' leather strap.

I got a second brother two months before my tenth birthday. He was named John. Just about then, pound, shilling and pence was replaced by dollars and cents.

By my eleventh birthday I had a fair amount of hair on my pelvis and under my arms, and my breasts had begun to grow. Then shortly after that, daddy took my virginity.

Chapter 3

By now I was completely at ease with daddy's kisses and caresses, and fiercely proud of the pleasure I could give him by using my hands and mouth on his manhood. I was still calling him 'daddy' though I now saw him as lover and patron. He wasn't hurting me, and was giving me true pleasure, so seeing that he wasn't my real daddy I saw nothing wrong with being his lover – especially since we weren't having sexual intercourse. Plus, as he had assured me, his loving and my eating of his sperm were making me grow real fast and pretty. Lately momma and almost every adult I knew were constantly commenting on how fast and pretty I was growing.

Two years ago, before daddy began loving me, I wasn't the tallest in my class. But now at eleven, I was indeed the tallest, having out-grown my classmates who had been taller than me when I was nine. (So how could my immature mind have seen anything wrong with loving daddy, I, who was so obsessed with growing up?)

I don't remember ever, up to then, thinking about the fact that daddy was momma's husband. I didn't wonder about their love-making, and I wasn't jealous when I saw them hugging and kissing. My main joy in being daddy's lover was the fact that I was convinced our loving was helping me to grow fast and extra pretty; the pleasure I got was only of secondary importance.

Looking back now from my mature stage in life I am moved to wonder if I would've reacted the same way if Mr Harry had been my real father. I am tempted to say no, I wouldn't have enjoyed incest and would've complained to momma after his first advance. Yes, I am moved to say that, even in the face of my obsession with growing up fast, I would not have succumbed to incest. But on the other hand I must admit that it is rather easy for a shrewd adult to get a child to engage in almost any act that doesn't cause the child any great pain, even if the child has been taught

14

that the act is wrong, especially when the adult is somebody dear to the child.

When daddy took my virginity I did know what incest was, but I wasn't even his legally adopted child. So, even now that I am a grown woman and regret that I was ever his lover, I never did see having sex with my stepdaddy as incest.

On an overcast Friday night momma went to a set-up leaving me and my two brothers with daddy, who had voiced and feigned weariness. Momma was glad she was able to leave us at home with daddy. If he was going to the set-up or to a bar, momma would've had to take us with her or leave us with a neighbour, and either case would've forced her to return home early. Daddy even grumbled as if he didn't want momma to go, but I knew he was glad she was going, and, of course, he and I knew that nothing less than a tragedy could have prevented momma from going to that particular set-up – the dead was one of the best bass voices our district had ever known.

Momma left at 8:00 p.m. looking very pretty in a knee-length pale pink dress, her oval face and large eyes bright with expectations of a truly lively set-up.

By nine o'clock my brothers, now aged five and two were asleep in the bed I shared with them. Daddy and I went to his and momma's bedroom. As usual he undressed me first and then himself. The lamp was turned down low and the curtains drawn. In the distant east I heard the soft rumble of thunder.

"Tonight we have real sex," daddy said leaning over me. I was lying on the edge of the bed, and his words caused me to gasp incredulously (he had never suggested he would someday claim my virginity). Then I was gaping at him with fear, surely his large seven-inch manhood would rip me apart? He saw that I was scared and whispered soothingly, "Don't be afraid my lovely little dove, my love. Surely by now yu know I wouldn't ever hurt yu. Now that yu start to grow hair on yu front an' yu breasts beginning to grow," (he was now on the bed caressing my rigid body), "yu is big enough fo' sex. I know how to make sure yu don't feel no pain. Trust me."

15

What could I do but trust him? Especially seeing that he fed my ego by adding, "Real sex will really mek' yu breasts develop fast."

He tied one of momma's scarves around my waist, real tightly, so that it was cutting into my flesh: this, he explained, would help to stretch my vagina. Then he rubbed petroleum jelly on his erect penis and spread two of his old pants on the bed for me to lie on so that my blood wouldn't mess the bed. By now I was trembling. Though I trusted daddy not to hurt me, I was afraid, having heard so often that the first time was painful and bloody.

Daddy caressed and kissed me all over, but I remained stiff with fear and was finding the scarf around my waist uncomfortable. I lost some of my fear and felt a slight stir of pleasure when he began to tongue my crotch. I closed my eyes when he moved over me and pushed up my knees. Next moment I felt a brief and sharp stab of pain as he entered my virgin cunt with a forceful, yet gentle, and skilled thrust. Then he was moving gently, and my first fuck became pleasurable but with a slight underlying discomfort that kept me from passing over into the nerve shattering state of climax.

Later on in life I was to learn that my stepfather had been forced to leave Portland by the wrath of his home district, including his family, after he was caught in the act of deflowering the ten year-old daughter of his second cousin. It was obvious that the girl had been willing to give up her virginity, so the police weren't called in. But daddy had received a beating at the hands of angry neighbours and relatives and told that he had best leave the area real soon. He hastily sold his possessions and came to Belfield. And his cousins in Belfield had kept the secret well, so that momma never had any reason to doubt his integrity.

After our first act of sexual intercourse I began to enjoy sex with daddy and was sure that the loss of my virginity was responsible for the rapid development of my body, which was now losing its girlish plumpness.

Daddy and I made love in various positions and places when-

ever the chance arose – in bed, on the floor, in a thick clump of wild-berry on his farm, at the seaside. He taught me the secrets of the male body, and by now I was very skilled. By the time I was thirteen he said I was a better lover than momma. (This compliment didn't please me because by then I was beginning to have a vague feeling that I was betraying momma.)

Many men, young and old, began to ask me who was my lover. I would feign anger and insist that I was a virgin or I would simply ignore them with histrionic disdain, when in fact I was proud of being the object of such a great mass of lust. Only a man's sperm, they all insisted, could cause a girl to develop so quickly.

Wherever I went, boys and men were begging me for sex. But I had no intention of seeking another lover. Daddy had told me that they wouldn't be as gentle as he was and would tell their friends all about me. In between my bouts of sex with daddy I satisfied my insatiable lust by masturbating and using small corncobs wrapped in plastic as dildoes. I felt no guilt about masturbating because daddy, whose words I saw as gospel, had told me that the taboos linked to it were false.

At about the time daddy took my virginity, two of my friends began to brag about having lost theirs. Their bragging began during the morning recess at school on a humid Monday. Our school, built on a small hilltop, was two long, parallel, rectangular one-storey buildings joined together by ten-foot walls across the end of the narrow space between them.

"Yu girls notice anything different 'bout me?" Winsome Ellis said jauntily. About six of us girls from Grade 5, aged ten to twelve, were in a secluded group in the small grassless front-yard eating mangoes that we had just bought from vendors at the gate. Half the twenty-minute recess was already gone.

"Different?" Mary Hinds queried humourously. "Yu in a new bouggas that too big fo' yu little foot."

This got some giggles.

Winsome pushed up her flat chest and screwed up her black face. "Not funny. I jus' meant to tell yu girls I am now a woman."

She shifted into a black American tone, "No longer a virgin, sugars. Get me?"

There was a brief silence, several mango-stained mouths hung open.

"So what?" Moreen Wright said with indifference, a retrospective smile on her half-Indian face. "I lost mine a year ago." I was the only one present who was taller than her.

"Eh-aa," petite Joy Jones ejaculated softly. "A wha' kind a talk this today." She was bare-footed and looked like a delicate doll in our blue uniform.

"Is nothing to shame 'bout," Winsome said defiantly. "Yu going to lose your own someday."

"Yes," Joy agreed, "But me no ready yet. Me a still pickney."

"Yu a child," Moreen said. "But not me."

I was tempted to declare that I wasn't a virgin, but common sense told me that if I did all the young men in an out of school would soon know about it, just as they soon knew that Winsome and Moreen were no longer virgins. "I a finish school first," I said.

Within a few weeks I was thanking my lucky stars that I had wisely refrained from telling my friends that I was no longer a virgin, and praised daddy for having warned me that if the boys and young men were to become certain that I was no virgin they would increase their pestering and feel free to hold and touch me on the streets. It wasn't long before the young men began to swarm my two braggart friends, Winsome and Moreen, wherever they went and often fondled them at school and on the street. This caused their boyfriends to get into several fights.

That's how our community was – and I suspect it still is the same – once it was known for sure that a girl was no longer a virgin, every male wanted to have sex with her before she became an 'old-hand' or had her first baby.

I began having my periods just before my thirteenth birthday. By then I had a thick patch of hair on my front and had to be shaving my underarms, and momma had already bought me my first two bras. I was now aware that our society and the law were

against a grown man like daddy having sex with a girl who was legally under-age. Daddy could go to prison, I mused, and I to a girls' home because I hadn't complained to momma; this knowledge alarmed me. Also I was now troubled by a vague feeling that daddy and I were doing momma a grave wrong and felt guilty after each act of love-making. But half of me was sure that such a pleasurable act couldn't be wrong. Plus, I reasoned, I wasn't a christian. So why did I now feel guilty after making love with daddy?

But on the other hand, I wondered, why did I melt whenever daddy took me in his arms, and knew only pleasure while we made love? He wasn't my real daddy, so we weren't committing incest like Mr Brown and his daughters.

Like a drug addict, I was hooked on daddy's loving and had no intention of seeking other lovers. Daddy and my corn-cob dildoes were enough.

Momma reminded me that I was now capable of having babies, but that as a 'real nice young lady' I was still too young for sex. "Don't go to lonely spots with boys and men," momma again warned sternly, "and take no gifts from them."

"Young girls like yu," she continued gravely, "usually die in child-birth. Those who live have to drop out of school. I was seventeen when yu was born and still it was so painful I was sure a was going to die." She gave a mock shudder of dread. We were in the kitchen preparing dinner on a week-day. I was now in the second day of my first period. "Plus," momma added wistfully, "a wouldn't want yu to have a child whose real father disown it."

I felt a great pity for her. In my young heart I knew it must be a terrible experience for a woman when her lover disowns his child. I promised momma I would continue to be a good girl, a real nice young lady. What would she do, I thought, if she found out that daddy and I were lovers? The thought made me both amused and ashamed, leaving me bewildered, as I now often was whenever I thought of my affair with daddy.

Daddy now began to use condoms when we made love – in

19

those days the pill wasn't as available as now, and, in any case, it would've been too risky to be on the pill without momma finding out sooner or later.

"A love yu," daddy said, "so a want yu to finish school an' find a nice husband before yu start have babies. The boys an' the other men 'bout here wouldn't care 'bout whether or not they get yu pregnant. Then when yu get pregnant they disown the belly. So yu must continue to keep away from them."

I disliked the feel of condoms inside me and it seemed wiser to just nurse on daddy's manhood. So more and more we began to engage in mostly oral sex, which daddy didn't mind. (I think momma disliked oral sex.) I was still convinced that sperm aided growth and appearance of a young girl's body, even though I was puzzled by the fact that my friend Winsome, who had many lovers, was roughly the same size she was when she had lost her virginity two years ago.

Perhaps Winsome wasn't developing fast, I thought, because she was getting too many different sperms. Or perhaps she was one of those persons who were born to be small and sadly flat-chested.

Shortly after my thirteenth birthday I was almost raped by one of the district's mad men, who was called Egg Eyes. He was about twenty-five years old and jet-black with large bulging eyes, short and stout, well fed by his large family, and lived by himself in a shack near the river. We often saw him when we went to wash clothes at the river and when momma occasionally allowed me to go shrimp fishing with friends. He was usually no threat to anyone, and he walked with a slight limp.

On a windy Thursday afternoon, I was on my way to buy some rice, my mind on the fact that the following night would be movie-night – a travelling 'show-man' showed movies at the school each night – and daddy had promised to take us all. Upon reaching a deserted section of the main road I was startled by Egg Eyes' sudden appearance out of the banana field above the road – he jumped down off the five-foot high embankment with his usual silly grin

on his face. I am sure he would've passed me if a strong wind had not suddenly blown my short skirt up above my waist. His eyes seemed ready to pop out of their sockets, and he got a good view of my red underwear before I hastily pulled down the hem of my skirt after a confused fumble. "Sister, yu thing fat!" Egg Eye exclaimed passionately. "Beg yu piece!" He was scratching his low uncombed dirt-matted hair; his sparse whiskers and beard were much cleaner.

Fear had transfixed me. He moved towards me smacking his thick lips lustfully. His overalls were filthy, his arms very dirty, teeth filthy. My legs were frozen and I was dumb, rooted. When the gap between us had closed to about eight feet I came to life, turned and fled.

His limp didn't slow him. The sound of his heavy boots was close behind me, loud on the asphalt. (I was barefoot and no slow runner.)

After the first twenty yards I knew he was really close behind me. Just then we began to move around a slight bend in the road. I felt his finger tips brush against my dress. An ear-splitting scream sprang from my throat and I lost my grip on the small paper bag and money in my hands.

Panic, caused by the feel of his fingers against the back of my dress, caused me to turn off the road into the banana/cocoa field below the road – there was no fence. I lost my footing and fell head over heels. Then Egg Eyes sprang on top of me and we rolled over and over down the gently slope, I kicking and screaming, he with firm grips on my shoulders and laughing. We came to rest against a sturdy nest of banana plants, Egg Eyes on top tearing at my clothes. But a second later two men were dragging him off me. He broke free and bolted down the slope.

My rescuers were two middle-aged men I knew well. One was daddy's good friend, and he took off his shirt and helped me into it. I was trembling and was unable to speak.

Two days later Egg Eyes was held by the police and locked away. Since then he was not seen back in Belfield.

Everyone, including myself, was shocked that Egg Eyes had done such a thing. He was usually so quiet and withdrawn. His family reacted towards me with kindness. But for several months I had some scary nightmares about him chasing me.

By the time I was fourteen, everyone said that I was the district's number one young beauty. I had inherited momma's even-toned medium-brown complexion and oval face with large glittering eyes. But I had inherited my father's short and sharp nose, and was already as tall as momma, and I had been blessed with a very sensuous bow of a mouth, with lips that were naturally red and neither too thick nor thin.

Momma said it would've been better if I had had less good looks and more brains; she was very disappointed that I had failed all the government exams. "I never see any other girl or woman," momma often said, "who so lucky to have both a very pretty face and such a good figure. Maybe yu will be able to win the Miss Jamaica crown."

Yes, at fourteen I had, and knew it, a superb figure that I haven't since lost. My bust was heavy, yet right for my height, and matched the generous swell of my hips and buttocks. My legs long and very delicate at the ankle.

Wherever I went the men of all ages couldn't hide their lust. But although I was thrilled to be the object of such lust, I refrained from being saucy or prim. In behaviour and dress, I was always modest in public.

After school on an overcast Thursday evening momma sent me and my older brother to the shop. As we neared the shop my brother stopped off at his friend's home. I went on alone, and there were no customers in the airy shop when I entered. The tall, burly, black, khaki-clad, middle-aged shopkeeper was dozing behind the board counter. He was jerked awake by a heavy rumble of thunder and lightning.

The shop's floor was concrete, and the board walls were painted and darkened by age. But it was one of the district's bigger and better shops. There was a bar to the left of the grocery area – all

was of board. It was the inheritance of the shopkeeper's Indian wife, and they had four teenaged children.

"Ah, the district beauty," Mr Reid said, his fleshy face glowing with lust. Behind his back he was known as 'Donkey-lengths' because he was said to have the largest manhood in the area – said to be as huge as a donkey's and had caused several women to he hospitalized over the years. He always wore khaki.

I blushed in the face of his candid lust. I glanced at the well-stocked shelves behind him.

"What fo' yu today?" he queried, scratching his thin hair. I named my few wants – flour, sugar and butter. He was silent while he served me. Then as I gave him the money, the rain came pouring down in a thick sheet. He made my change and came from behind the counter. I packed the items in my bag.

"How old yu be now?" He was standing close to me, gazing down with open lust: he was over six feet tall.

"Fourteen," I said, suddenly feeling nervous but determined not to show it.

He held my bare arm caressingly. "Old enough to do as yu please. And big enough to please any man."

"Mr Reid," I said truly shocked. "Suppose yu wife come see us."

"She an' the kids not here."

I gulped nervously as his fingers caressed my arm. "Somebody might come into the shop."

"Not in this rain. So what? Yu would mek' me sex yu?"

I pulled away from him. "No!" He was the last man I would want!

"A know what scaring yu." He sighed dejectedly, leaning against the counter. "Yu believe that lie about me thing big like donkey."

Silence. The sound of the rain on the ceiling-less zinc roof and my pulse were loud in my ears.

"Don't believe them things," he said after endless seconds of thought. "Me is a normal man. And a will give yu anything to sex yu. What yu say about now if a lock the shop?"

Suddenly, I was angry. "No! A would never want a married man!" The irony of this statement softened my glare and tone. "If I ever to have sex in here it must be with yu son."
He began to laugh. The rain lessened and I fled. But in my soul I was wondering what it would be like to have sex with a man whose manhood was bigger than daddy's but not as large as a donkey's. In the not too distant future I was to meet a man whose manhood was almost as huge as a young donkey's.

One of my grandaunts died four months before my fifteenth birthday. So, of course, we all went to the set-up. The night was moonless and starry and cool. The day, a Saturday, had been very hot but now in the night there was a steady, humid, soft breeze blowing off the sea. My grandaunt had been popular in our district and also in the neighbouring districts, so there was a vast turnout of people at the set-up.

The 'dead-yard' was about a quarter of a mile from my home, on a level parcel of land on the main road. The singing booth (bamboo frame, without walls, with canvas roof) had been made adjoining the verandah at the front of the five-room board house. An electric bulb hung low over the hymn-reader's chair at the table in the centre of the booth. At about eleven o'clock, when the singers were in full stride and everyone was anticipating the feast which would be served near midnight, I allowed two boys from the class above mine to lead me away from a group of my girlfriends and cousins near the booth. We were singing to the hymns.

"Carlene we hav' a secret yu won't want to miss," Barry said.

"Yea," Calvin intoned, "only yu mus' hear this."

"I want to hear," I assured them, "But we not going anywhere lonely."

"Just over there so," Calvin said, pointing to a low Julie mango tree along the fence, his round face cunning.

"Carlene, why yu don't run them?" one of my cousins said, "A somebody them a look."

"I'll soon be back," I said, moving off with the boys. I knew

24

their plan was to try to seduce me by fondling and sweet words when we arrived in the semi-darkness under the mango tree. But I was sure I would leave them frustrated after teasing them for a few minutes. I was feeling real mischievous. And both boys had been my most persistent admirers over the past few months. Apparently, they had decided that their best chance of getting sex from me was to work together, since it was obvious I didn't love either one of them. Well, tonight I was going to show them, I thought, that I just was not interested in casual sex with boys.

Momma and daddy were in the thick group of singers and didn't see me walking away with Calvin and Barry. As soon as we arrived under the mango tree I sat down on a piece of log lying on the ground. The boys sat down on either side of me. The low branches, the bamboo fence behind us and the dim light hid our movements from prying eyes. The singing surged at us.

"Yu boys think I fool?" I said, before they could speak. "I know yu have no secret to tell me."

"So yu want our loving," Barry said excitedly, moving closer. He was a short and slim half-Indian. Mouse-faced.

"Eh, it look like she feel seh one a we wouldn't good enough," Calvin said confidently, moving closer and pushing a hand up under my skirt. He was short, thick-set and black.

For two minutes I silently allowed them to fondle my front and fight with my bra – I was wearing a sweater. Then an idea hit me, causing my juices to flow. Ignoring their pleas to follow them to the bushes behind the house, I surprised them with swift movements of my hands to open their zippers and reaching inside their underwear to take firm hold of their erect pricks. I now became oblivious to the singing.

They gasped in surprise and their hands froze on my body.

"Surrender or I shall break off your pricks," I teased and began to masturbate them. At first they tried to move away, but I held them firmly, and they were already so aroused that the next moment were overcome by ecstasy. Silently they moved closer to me, and I increased the tempo of my wanking. And though

their hands had stopped caressing me, I was ecstatic – it was truly a glorious feeling to be holding two throbbing pricks.

They didn't last long, Calvin first, climbing half-way to his feet and grunting through clenched teeth. Then Barry came, hanging onto my neck and gasping. I wiped my hands on the grass at my feet and, before the boys had recovered half their wits, I said: "If you boys ever ask me for sex again, I am going to tell your friends about tonight." I walked away, leaving them with heads hung in shame. Thereafter, they were errand boys, but never so much as mentioned the word sex in my hearing: the threat of having their friends learn about my masturbating them was as deadly as a loaded gun.

When I turned fifteen, I knew, and not just because men and women often told me so, that I was definitely the most beautiful and sexiest young woman in our district, one of that small percentage of women who will always turn heads in a crowd. All my childhood fat was gone and replaced by sleek, naturally well-toned muscles. Whenever I surveyed myself in a mirror the only fault I could find with my appearance was that my eyes were a bit too large.

I began to seriously consider my mother's and relative's claim that I could do well in any major beauty contest. To this end they insisted that I should always wear shoes and take active interest in the news on the radio and in the newspaper. Daddy was also excited by the prospect of me being a beauty queen, so he made sure I had extra shoes, bought the week-end papers and began to give serious thought to increasing his earnings to be able to send me to high school. He was also adamant that I should wash my hair with the aloe-vera plant because, he insisted, it was far superior to all commercial shampoos. (In childhood, carrying water on my head had made my hair coarse, short and listless, but since we had received a pipe in our yard two years ago – 1973 – my hair had began to soften, grow and show life.)

However, though I was attracted by the idea of entering a beau-

ty contest, I didn't see being a beauty queen as a great accomplishment. I was aware of all the glitter attached to it, but to me, it seemed pointless for a group of girls to be pitting their looks against each other. After all, I mused, beauty is basically a God-given legacy. Was it right to engage legacies given by God in a contest? Which wasn't the same as using God's gifts to better one's life. Instead of entering a beauty contest it seemed to me that it would indeed be nobler if I used my beauty to get a rich husband or a good job.

By now I was convinced that sex with daddy was a sin against momma. And though I was still enjoying our love-making, in my soul I did want to end the affair. Thus it wasn't strange that I fell in love with Kevin, a handsome Kingstonian, as soon as he came to visit his aunt that summer.

Kevin's aunt lived next door to my home and was momma's good friend. On the first day of his visit he passionately declared that I was the sexiest girl he had ever seen, and marvelled that I had developed so much since his last visit two years ago. His gallant compliment caused me to get so aroused that I immediately knew he would be my second lover.

But I couldn't have foreseen the many horrid and dark events that would be unleashed by taking him as my true love.

Chapter 4

Kevin's parents had managed to coax and bribe him into coming to live with his aunt 'Dimples' for an unlimited period of time so as to keep him out of the political violence that had flared up in Kingston since the beginning of the year. It was also hoped that he would lose his love for guns and the company of gunmen in and around the Waltham Park area where his family lived. Kevin's parents were lower middle class and devoted christians.

Kevin Edwards had just sat his G.C.E. 'O' Level exams before he came on this visit at the beginning of the summer of 1975. He had been attending Trench Town High and had no intention of furthering his education as yet. His great love was guns, but I didn't know this in that summer.

His Aunt Dimples, Mrs Grey, was his mother's younger sister. The Greys lived next door to our home. The two houses were separated by about a chain of banana/cocoa plants, which was owned by the Greys, our house being very close to the boundary. Dimples was a short, plump, black cheerful thirty-year-old. She was an open and kind-hearted soul. Her husband was a thirty-four year-old carpenter/mason, a short muscular black man who loved children. They had four children; the oldest, a boy, was the same age as the older of my two brothers.

In the past, Kevin's visits were short and, being two years older than me and a bit of a celebrity, his being from Kingston, he took very little notice of me. As soon as he came he would be flocked by the older girls who were willing to have sex with him. I had always admired him but I wasn't the type of girl who could love a man who showed very little interest in her.

But now in the summer of '75 he instantly saw that I was a woman and the number one beauty around.

"Carlene you are the sexiest girl I ever see," he had said passionately when we met on the Friday afternoon he arrived. We met on my way home from school, and he and I were standing

close together and off by ourselves. "Carlene my girl," he continued with charm, as I stood blushing, "you really grow these two years a don't see you. And I say it again, you are the sexiest girl I ever see." His black face glowed.

Ecstasy dazed me. My pussy began to dampen with love juice. And I felt the first warm tugging of love on my racing heart. To be paid such a compliment by a handsome high school graduate from Kingston was a great honour for me, who had one more year left before graduating from our dreary primary school. (In those days, we country folks were in great awe of Kingstonians, so a compliment from Kevin was valuable to any girl in our area, even if she was a high school graduate.) Still, feminine pride forced me to say, "That's what yu tell all the girls." My voice was husky and I couldn't stop myself from smiling as I searched his handsome face. "An' yu never expect that I was going to grow like all them bigger girls yu always have time for?" I now cocked my head saucily, still searching his black face.

He grinned good-naturedly. "I really mean what a said about you being the sexiest girl," he said seriously. "Now, I won't try to deny that I use to give you only very little of my time. But from now on you'll see that I will be paying you much more attention than I have ever paid any other girl."

" So yu say." My voice was unsteady and I knew that my face was now fully flushed. Love swelled my heart and my nipples were straining against my bra, and my love juice was flowing like a stream.We walked off.

There was one week to go before our school closed for summer. Kevin walked me home after school each day, telling me witty tales and saying nothing about sex or love. I was proud of his awaiting me at the school gate each afternoon, and I refused to share his company with any of my girlfriends. Each afternoon I was aware of their envious eyes. Their envy and desire even made them refrain from asking me much about my relationship with Kevin.

Like myself, none of the girls at school had interested Kevin before now. The girls whom he used to court up to his former visit

two years ago were now either in senior high school or had graduated from school. He was truly the 'handsome young man.' Tall and trim with athletic looks. He was now seventeen, hair was just beginning to grow on his chin and cheeks; a slightly arrogant chin and a determined tilt to the slightly hollow jaw. His complexion was a smooth black, and his handsome face was always pleasantly lit by his wide-set eyes and ever-ready smile. He moved gracefully, agile and confident. The only boy of five children born close together, he truly understood girls.

Summer holidays came and Kevin was all mine by day, ignoring all his former conquests and admirers. (I was sure he went in search of sex at nights.) He was always at my home or I at his aunt's. Whenever momma sent me to the shops he went with me. His radiant smiles, pleasing manners and intelligent speech – and of course because he was momma's friend's nephew – made momma approve of our seemingly harmless friendship.

Momma was sure Kevin was too refined a gentleman to pressure me for sex; poor momma had never been good at judging people correctly. But I knew he was only buying time before beginning to coax me for sex. I was ready to give him my body when he asked, and was praying that my sexual skill would go a long way in influencing him to fall head-over-heels in love with me.

"Don't, " momma admonished me, "tempt him with your body. He is not a little boy anymore."

Momma and I still didn't know, had no reason to suspect, that Kevin was a budding gunman. Kevin's Aunt Dimples kept this fact secret from us, and Kevin didn't mention guns or gunmen friends to me.

Kevin's aunt had always had a special love for me. Now she casually encouraged my relationship with Kevin, giving me subtle warnings to use ample protection if we intended to have sex. Looking back, I now think she was hoping he would fall in love with me and decide to remain in the country – this would have suited his family's campaign to keep him away from guns and political gunmen.

30

Needless to say, daddy was jealous. Of course, I had expected him to be. Though I would've loved to tell him that I was in love with Kevin, I thought it would be best to tell him that I had no intimate interest in Kevin. "I have no intention of having sex with Kevin," I coaxed daddy after we made love one night when momma was away. But in fact I was yearning for Kevin, had pretended that it was he instead of daddy who had just steered me to a shattering climax, and I was longing to tell daddy that I wanted to end our immoral affair. At nights when I masturbated or used my corn-cob wrapped in plastic it was Kevin whom I thought about. Would Kevin be bigger than daddy ? Was he a good lover?

Daddy was no fool. He suspected that I did love Kevin. "If him really love yu, him will still want yu a few years from now when him or the two a yu working," daddy said evenly, ignoring my claim of disinterest in Kevin. "Yu mustn't lie down with a young man who can't or won't support a family." We were getting dressed in the semi-dark bedroom. "Plus," he added solemnly, "yu still going to school, an' young boys like Kevin should get practice from the older girls an' big women."

Though my love for Kevin was making my affair with daddy less pleasing, it felt good to be the cause of jealousy.

Whenever it was possible, Kevin and I kissed and fondled each other. At the end of the second week of his visit he asked me if I would have sex with him.

" Yes," I said huskily, squeezing his hand. We were sitting on his Aunt's verandah on a scorching afternoon – we were very close on the wide patio canvas chair. His aunt was in the kitchen twenty feet to the side of the five-room board house. My brothers and his cousins – all scantily clad – were playing marbles in the small grassless frontyard. I was in shorts and T- shirt.

"I have some boots," he said with a happy grin, referring yo condoms, showing his lovely teeth, "so you won't have to worry about getting pregnant." He squeezed my leg.

Faking anger I snapped, "You came prepared to deal with all the girls here." I was doing my best to speak as well as he, though

at times he did lapse into patois. I was searching his twinkling eyes.

"A few," he admitted softly, and my love for him grew because I preferred the truth always.

"But Carlene," he added with a soft gaze, "because a love you I am not interested in loving anyone but you from now on. Forever."

Love gripped my heart and I oh so wanted to believe his romantic words. I gave him a provocative gaze. Did he truly love me, or just after my pussy?

"I love you," he whispered passionately. "Only you."

"I love you too," I said earnestly, ecstasy washing over me.

Because my brothers and Kevin's cousins followed us wherever we went, he and I were unable to have sex during the days. We tried but couldn't shake off the younger kids, especially his four-year-old girl cousin whom he adored as much as she worshipped him. And momma just wouldn't allow me out of the yard at nights.

But, as the popular saying goes, where there is a will there is always a way.

Our first encounter – that's how I now see our first act of sex – was in my toilet in the fourth week of Kevin's visit, about the 20th of July.

At about 8:00 p.m. on a clear, starry, moonless night – either a Tuesday or a Wednesday – I asked my brothers to come with me to our out-house pit-toilet. I lit a kerosene 'bottle-lamp' and we went outside, leaving momma and daddy in the hall listening to the radio. As soon as I came out onto the verandah I began to sing 'Sweet Jesus', my signal to Kevin to go into the toilet – and made sure my brothers didn't pass me when I paused on the low rough concrete front steps.

Light from the street-light half a chain above our locked gate cast eerie shadows across our small grassless front-yard. There had been electricity on our lane for sometime now, but daddy

couldn't afford to wire our house as yet. Still singing 'Sweet Jesus', I preceded my brother down the gentle slope to our back-yard and left them with the bottle lamp a fair distance from the toilet – a sturdy and clean zinc structure about six by seven feet.

The night was warm and, except for the sound of night insects, still.

I entered the dark toilet with breathless anticipation. Kevin was waiting with an old blanket spread on the dyed board floor. I closed the door. And we lay down trembling with weeks of desire.

I was wearing no underwear and he was clad only in black briefs. We didn't have time for foreplay and because my brothers were near we had to be silent.

But inside the dark toilet seemed like heaven when he entered me.

By necessity it was hurried. But it was also delightful and satisfying. I experienced the quickest orgasm I had ever had. I was tempted to stay for a second bout, but I was afraid that momma and/or daddy might've suspected something was wrong.

Later in my bed, I used my corn-cob dildo, whispering Kevin's name, and then dreamt that we had just been married and were making love in our wedding attire.

By now everyone knew I was Kevin's 'official girl'. But, of course, like everybody else, I knew he still had lovers whom he sought by night. Several girls on my lane began to give me malicious looks because they resented my monopoly of Kevin by day.

Two days after our encounter in the toilet, Kevin's aunt got a television – their house had been wired some time before – and momma allowed me and my brothers to go watch it at nights, but not past 10 o'clock.

Kevin and I had decided that the toilet meeting was too confined and risky. So a few days later I began to sneak out of the house after midnight.

The room I shared with my brothers had a back door that led onto the small landing on top of the back steps. Thankfully, the back door opened noiselessly. On the nights when Kevin and I

intended to meet, I tied a long piece of cord to my big toe after my brothers fell asleep. Then I hung the other end of the cord through a small space left between the bottom of the window's movable half and the ledge by my single bed; my brothers shared a bigger bed which was by the other window. When Kevin came, anywhere between midnight and 2:00 a.m., he pulled the cord to waken me.

I always came awake as soon as Kevin tugged on the cord. Then I silently crept from the room. Thank heavens we didn't have any dogs to yap about; daddy didn't like dogs and momma wasn't exactly a dog lover.

I never felt any fear when leaving the house, but did experience some anxiety upon the return journeys. Kevin and I made love on an old blanket and old coats spread on the ground in the banana field behind our toilet. We always spent at least an hour together; Kevin always had his watch.

The first night was one and a half hours of pure bliss under a clear and starry sky, with an old half moon shining down on our naked bodies. I had about five orgasms, he three.

Although Kevin wasn't as skilled a lover as daddy, there was a special pleasure in our love-making – because I was in love with Kevin, the satisfaction he gave me seemed to linger all through the next day. He used condoms so I was denied the glory of feeling his seed spill inside me; I wasn't willing to risk getting pregnant, much as I loved him, but I always drank his seed from the condom and sometimes 'blew' him – I was disappointed that he refused to eat my pussy.

I knew he was surprised at my sexual skills, but all he said was that I was the best he ever had.

We met at least twice each week. And I was soon convinced that he really was in love with me.

How wrong I was! I now feel that he was one of those young men who was incapable of falling in love.

Momma allowed me to go to a dance with Kevin on Independence night. My first real date and dance – in the past I always went to the dances on special holidays with momma and daddy but wasn't allowed into the dancing area.

The dance was at our primary school and there had been a fair there in the day. At the fair Kevin and I had been the most admired couple.

It was about 8:30 p.m. when I went into the dark, half-packed dance area, feeling a very proud woman. Kevin looked real breathtaking in his blue three-piece suit; I was in a red knee-length satin dress that hugged my figure. Clutching our beers we went to lean against the wall at the back of the long narrow high-roofed ceilingless hall. Then we embraced each other and began to do the rub-a-dub to the bassy reggae music. By the time the hall became crowded at 9 o'clock I had had two orgasms.

At about 9:15 p.m. we left the noisy hot and jam-packed dance hall. We went across to the crowded bar where momma and daddy were at a table with friends – most of the people sitting in the brightly illuminated bar were adults over thirty years old.

The bar was just a temporary set-up in the woodwork room, cleared of the work benches and tools. After buying our beers and saying hello to momma and daddy – he avoided my eyes – Kevin and I went next door to the kitchen and bought two cups of the steaming 'mannish water – soup'. Then with him carrying the soup and me bearing our two beers we left the school building.

Outside was cool. My sweaty body began to feel less sticky. We went around to the school's dark back-yard and found a secluded spot away from the few entwined couples lying or sitting on the ground. Kevin spread his large towel on the grass and we sat down. From this distance the music sounded much more mellow and clear.

After drinking our soup in silence, I confessed to him the fact that I had had two orgasms while we were dancing – we had danced only in the rub-a-dub style, pelvis grinding against pelvis.

"It was a sin to let myself go," I added, sincerely penitent, "while you were unable to."

"You are so strange," he said with amusement and tightened his embraced. "There is no need for you to feel guilty about letting yourself go in a dance. That's a girl's privilege."

"Anyway," I said provocatively, "I am now going to make it up to you." I took off his jacket and pulled his pants. Then with him half-reclining on his elbows, I 'blew' him under the starry sky, with its half-moon looking down on us, the music flowing from the school building and the sounds of insects in the nearby bushes urging me on.

Afterwards he lit a cigarette and began to drink his beers – I had had one beer already and now decided that I shouldn't drink another.

"Should've bought you a soda," he said, contentedly blowing smoke.

"I am alright. A don't really like sodas." I moved onto his lap. "I just drink the last mouthfuls of each beer."

He threw away his cigarette – up to then I didn't even suspect that he smoked marijuana; not that I would've loved him any less if I had known, seeing that I knew so many kind and gentle persons who smoked the 'weed'.

"I hope you won't mind my asking," he said simply, the wise look on his face was plain in the soft moonlight. "You don't have to answer. But I must ask it, which man teach you so much about sex?"

For weeks I had been prepared for this question. Without meeting his eyes I leaned against his chest and asked, "You sorry I wasn't a virgin fo' yu?"

"I wouldn't want a virgin for my wife. If you was a virgin I would a did have to waste time teaching you the basics. Me no like virgins."

He sounded sincere. And truly mature. My heart was racing with excitement. Did his mention of a wife mean that he loved me so much as to see me as his future wife?

I glanced up into his face, but just then a cloud passed over the moon and plunged us into real darkness; so I couldn't be sure just what I had seen in his shadowy eyes. Once more I lowered my head against his chest. "At the end of last year, I had a nineteen-year-old boyfriend," I lied in a hesitant tone. "We broke up. I won't tell you who he is. He once lent me a book with pictures and writing 'bout every type a sex." (Daddy had told me about such books.)

"Yeah," he said evenly. "A girl can learn nuff about sex from a book and a few fucks." He sighed. "You girls so lucky. It take a man years to learn to give a good fuck. Good thing I did start when a was ten. Me first teacher was a go-go dancer." He chuckled. "When me reach twelve, she shake me out a the pussy, straight off the bed, because I tell her to wind sweeter."

We both began to laugh.

A few minutes later we returned to the dance. Then shortly before 1:00 a.m. we left with momma and daddy – my brothers were with Kevin's aunt.

By now I was getting almost no pleasure from sex with daddy and felt very depressed after each act. Now that I was having sex with the man I loved, and now knew my affair with daddy was a great sin against momma, I wanted to stop being daddy's lover and be his daughter once more. But I just didn't know how to end the sordid affair without making daddy more jealous of Kevin; already I knew daddy was sure Kevin and I were lovers, sure that by day we were able to have sex under momma's nose. I was sure that if I stopped giving daddy my body he would begin to watch Kevin and me more closely, find out that I was leaving the house at nights and somehow kill my affair with Kevin.

As it was, fate intervened.

On a full-moon night momma awoke and saw that my bed was empty. She and daddy came outside. They caught Kevin and me rolling naked on a blanket behind the toilet.

Chapter 5

There is a popular Jamaican saying – 'Chicken merry, hawk deh near'. This saying amply describes that unforgettable night when momma and daddy caught Kevin and me 'red-handed'.

Kevin and I didn't hear momma's and daddy's approach. We couldn't have for we were far gone on the erotically ecstatic road towards our first orgasm of the night. And, indeed, I had sneaked out of the house in an exceptionally horny and merry state – very horny because I was nearing my period; exceptionally merry because Kevin had that evening said, "Will you someday be my wife?" His voice was soft and as romantic as the love song flowing from the little two-room board house across the street – we were standing at his aunt's gate at dusk, bathed by a street-light.

"Yes," I said breathlessly.

So, when at midnight he tugged at the cord attached to my big toe, I was already awake; and, feeling as mellow as the soft yellowish kerosene lamp-light, I was on the verge of easing some of my overwhelming desire by masturbating. Hastily, I had pulled the cord from my big-toe and tugged it inside. After a quick glance at my brothers' bed – they were literally asleep in each others arms – I noiselessly left the semi-dark room through the back-door. (I wonder if my brothers still, now that they are grown men, sleep as sound as they did as boys?) Kevin was waiting at the bottom of the seven-foot high steps. He looked so gloriously handsome in the moonlight. I tip-toed down the steps, jumped into his arms and gave him a brief devouring and somewhat dominating kiss. He tasted and smelt of smoke – not then knowing much about marijuana, I assumed it to be cigarette smoke, but I must now assume it could have also partly been of marijuana.

The night was cool, the brilliant light of the full moon gave my short, thin, cheap nightgown an expensive silky look. Kevin was in full black, pants and sweater. Hand in hand, we hurried to where he had left the blanket, old sheets and old coats all arranged

behind the toilet. Silently and frantically we stripped, then fell onto our makeshift bed.

It was now October, almost four months since Kevin had arrived. And, still not knowing about his love for guns and his family designs to change him, I believed his claim that I was the sole reason why he had remained in our district so long.

"It's going to be so hard to leave you," he had said one cloudy afternoon as we sat in his aunt's living room. "But I will have to go seek a job. No jobs here in the country for me."

"Then you'll forget me," I accused.

"Never. When you leave school I want you to come away with me."

Shortly after this, school had re-opened in September, and because I was the district's most attractive girl, in the graduate class and Kevin's girl I was the most popular and envied girl at school, the undisputed queen. With the coming of October, I began to worry about the coming rainy season, which would upset my night dates with Kevin. But the almost inevitable October rains had still not begun as yet as Kevin and I now made love, not knowing that momma and daddy were upon us.

I opened my eyes when I felt Kevin's body beerrforcefully dragged off mine. It was daddy, angry and silently yanking Kevin's naked, sweaty body away from mine. Fear killed my ecstasy and chilled me; the sweat on my naked body felt like ice-water; the cool sea breeze now felt deadly cold.

I wanted to die, wanted to flee. But could only gape. Then I saw momma. She stood nearby, staring wide-eyed at me, the moonlight filtering through the banana leaves above her head made eerie shadows on her pale-green nightgown; daddy's striped pajamas somehow looked vicious.

"Get off me land before a mash-up yu damn face!" daddy snarled at Kevin. Kevin's face showed fear. He scooped up his clothes and fled, the condom still on his limp prick. Me, I was now on my knees, trembling and – stupidly – trying unsuccessfully to get into my nightgown. Fear made me bewildered and scared of daddy.

Daddy turned his jealously angry face to me; in the yellowish moonlight his clean-shaven brown face was fiery flushed right down to his thick neck. He was about seven feet from me.

"Get up an' put on yu clothes!" daddy barked at me, fists angrily clenched at his side. The sight of those large fists made my skin crawl; I had the feeling that if his rage of jealously now overwhelmed him he would pummel me to death. And momma's gaping silence suggested that she would've stood by silently while he beat me to death.

Quivering with dread, I stood up and, avoiding their eyes, I fought my way into my nightgown.

"Carlene, why?" Momma stuttered softly and pathetic – perhaps she thought she was dreaming. "Why? ...How yu could..."

"A good beating is what she want, " daddy interjected vehemently. Then before I could react he was upon me and took a firm hold of my arm. Dazed by fear, I didn't resist – had no strength to command my quivering limbs – as he dragged me to a nearby tree and tore off a branch.

The first lash was across my back, and it jerked me out of my dazed state. I screamed and struggled but was unable to break free of his vice-like grip. He gave me about seven lashes before releasing me with a running-shot (a lash as I fled) across my buttocks. I fled to – where else – my bed.

My brothers were fast asleep. I lay there under my thin blanket, sobbing softly; my bottom, legs and arms seemingly on fire. I was seething with hatred for daddy. He was my mother's husband, I thought angrily, and old enough to have been my real daddy, so why should he want to be my only lover? In the first place he shouldn't ever have even thought of seducing me. Well, he would never again get the chance to even look at my cunt. And perhaps someday I would be able to avenge his cruelty to me.

As a Taurean, I had a lot of patience.

I saw neither momma nor daddy for the rest of that unforgettable night. I got little sleep. After musing on my hatred for daddy and my desire for vengeance, I began to think of running away.

But where was I going to run? Kevin was still living with his parents and might not find a job for quite a while.

But it would be so hard, I mused, to continue living here with momma and daddy. Would momma allow me to go live with one of my aunts? But what reason would I give for wanting to leave her home? Surely, I wouldn't be able to tell her that daddy and I had been lovers for years?

No, I decided, I couldn't do that. To tell her of my affair with daddy would only have caused her great grief and unhappiness. I had to stay on until I turned sixteen, then I would go live with my aunt at my grandparents' house, which had been willed to all their grandchildren born before their deaths.

And, of course, by the time I turned sixteen Kevin might be able to rent a home for us. I was glad daddy had not attempted to hit Kevin. I had best encourage Kevin to return to Kingston immediately. God knew what daddy's jealousy might still lead him to do.

After hours of thought I did drift into a deep dreamless sleep.

Next morning there were fat welts and small cuts all over my aching body, where daddy 's lashes had hit me. Oh, how I hated him! I was glad that he had left for work before I got out of bed.

A voice was urging me to tell momma that daddy had been my lover since age nine. But I didn't want to make her unhappy.

I knew it was only natural that daddy should be jealous of Kevin. But why beat me, especially with such a sturdy branch? What kind of man was he to expect to own both my mommas – his wife and my cunt? The beast! How I wished I had been sensible and strong enough to have spurned his sexual advances from that first night when I was nine.

At about 10:30 a.m. Momma led me to her room for a 'woman to woman talk'. (Since leaving my bed I had been avoiding her eyes.) We were alone at home – daddy gone to work; my brothers to school. Without being told I had known I wouldn't be expected to go to school. Now I sat down on momma's dressing-table stool. She sat on the bed. What could she do, I thought wistfully and

penitently, if she knew how many times her husband and I had made love on that bed.

The room was tidy and the windows open, the thin curtains tied aside to allow the gentle wind from off the sea to flow freely. The morning was cloudy, now the sun was bright, then a few seconds later it would dim its shine. The area was quiet, children already in school, workers long since on their jobs, housewives quiet. A few robins began to sing in the fields opposite our home.

I glanced at momma. Her face had aged, dark circles under the now listless eyes. She wet her lips and said, "Well Carlene, yu is a woman now." Her voice was even, but her eyes showed disappointment. These were her first words to me since morning. She sighed despondently and added hopefully, "A only hope yu not pregnant."

My eyes were downcast, hands tightly clasped in my lap, my mind blank.

"Carlene," momma continued, "a want yu to promise me yu will stay away from sex until after yu graduate from school next year. Promise?"

I nodded, eyes still downcast. A motorbike raced down our recently paved lane – the last quarter leading to the river had been left unpaved. A group of parakeets screamed past over our house as if they had been scared out of the banana/cocoa field across the road.

Momma heaved a huge sigh and shook her head dejectedly. Her short hair was tied with a colourful scarf and she wore a loose-fitting floral dress. My hair was untidy and I was wearing a long skirt and t-shirt.

"Alright," momma said with resignation, "a going to trust yu word. I really wish yu could put off sex for a few years. But since I birth yu when I was seventeen a can't tell yu not to have sex after yu reach sixteen next year. Yu will have to decide."

I felt empty and so weary.

"The reason a would advise yu to wait until yu is eighteen or nineteen is because a don't want yu to face what I face with yu as

a baby." Her voice was low and wistful. "Yu might feel sure Kevin love yu but it's too early to know." She sighed thoughtfully, her ample bosom rose and fell in slow motion; obviously she was searching for words. "Perhaps him even have a girl in Kingston. Woman musn't trus' man too easy. Yu have to be careful with man. Plus yu is still only a schoolgirl."

Silence. My eyes were still downcast, hands wringing. I shifted uneasily on the cushioned stool, the welts on my bottom smarting. The bike that had passed down earlier now roared past up the lane.

A suspended minute of silence passed before momma said, suddenly angry, "Imagine yu leave out of the house in the middle of the night."

Again she fell silent. When was she, I thought impatiently, going to allow me to go. Then my mind went blank once more. I had an odd feeling that momma and I were going to sit as we were for the rest of our lives, while the world stood still about us.

Momma sighed dolefully and I had to fight the urge to heave a sigh.

"Carlene, yu serious about not having sex again until after yu graduate?"

I nodded and took a quick peep at her distorted face.

"Tell me the truth," she coaxed. "Las' night was the first time?"

I nodded, eyes downcast, tongue as heavy as a lead.

"Look at me and answer!" momma snapped exasperatedly.

I glanced into her angry, searching eyes. "Yes," I whispered, then hastily lowered my eyes and rolled my buttocks uneasily. I thought I should stand, but I felt so weary and empty.

"Las' night was the first night yu leave out a the house?" momma persisted.

This time I could only nod.

"Yu lying! Is not the first time yu go out to Kevin in the night! I know when yu telling lie." She groaned mournfully. "That mean yu might be pregnant?"

"No," I whispered. It seemed wiser to speak the truth. I moist-

ened my dry lips. "Kevin always use protection." I was gazing at my wringing hands on my lap.

I heard her vent a long suffering sigh, and I could almost hear the shaking of her head I was sure accompanied that sigh. "At least a mus' say bless him fo' that," she said with tangible relief. Then for endless seconds there was a heavy and thick silence – I could have carved a slice.

Dear God, I prayed, please make her allow me to go now.

"Kevin is the first one?"

I knew I should say a quick and assuring yes, but for some unknown reason I hesitated long enough for her to see the truth. (Perhaps I, unconsciously, really did want her to see the truth. So that I could confess about daddy and me?) And I didn't get another chance to reply.

Momma sprang to her feet, steaming with rage, bosom dancing, her hope that it had been true love for Kevin why I had fallen from the hill of virginity was now shattered beyond salvage. Her first affair, with my real father, had been for love. The thought that I had given up my virginity due to lust and vanity was too much for her to bear. "Yu little bitch!" she cried vehemently. "How long since yu a leave out a the house go lie down with man! How long!" She towered over me, glaring. "How much man yu know before Kevin?"

I was dumb, transfixed. Gazing up at her, knowing I should get up and flee. But I was so weary and empty. And – believe this – sorry for her, ashamed that I had disappointed, and sinned against her. It only seemed right that she should flog me if she so wished. I also felt a strong urge to confront her, draw her against my young bosom; she seemed so pathetic, even though she was raving. The urge to comfort her was so strong that I ceased to feel the smarting of my welted bottom.

Momma rushed towards the thick leather strap hanging on a nail in the wall, where it always hung when out of use. Now I sprang to my feet with the intention of fleeing the room; as penitent and remorseful as I was, it no longer seemed rational to willingly accept a flogging on my already welted body.

But, it was too late to flee. She already had the strap and barred the way to the door with her stout, strong body. (It had been over two years since she had last flogged me.) With the strap raised high she rushed at me, and there wasn't much space in the room to dodge her. The strap bit into my shoulder. I screamed and thought of heading for the nearest of the two windows to jump through – they were only about five feet above the ground, but momma cut me off from both windows, cornered me neatly. And while she swung that thick strap with her full strength – she was a strong woman – she snarled, "Yu little bitch! ...How...long...yu a ...tek' man...Yu...little...bitch...?"

I was screaming for mercy. And I just couldn't force my way past her: each time I tried she used her strong hand and arm to push me back into the corner – she was as fleet-footed as a world-class boxer.

Then indignation flooded me swiftly. I stopped my screams for mercy. Her husband, a voice in my head screamed, taught you the joys of flesh. So why then flog you for making love with the young man whom you loved?

"Daddy was my first lover!" I shouted defiantly. Momma's hand froze in mid-flight. "Him tek' me virginity when a was eleven!" (I am now thanking God that nobody was passing on the street, which was only twenty-five feet away.)

Time stopped. The only sound was my heavy breathing as I glared at momma's drained face; she was gaping incredulously. The only movement was my heaving bosom. Momma was frozen, transfixed, a wax form, her hand and leather strap suspended above her head.

For several dark moments we stood thus, caught in the cobweb of our timely making, loving and hating each other. Then momma jerked into action like a missile just launched. Her left fist jabbed into my throat just as the right hand brought down the strap most powerfully across my smarting back.

I sank, crumpled, to my watery knees fighting for breath, clawing at my throat. Through the fog in my head I heard her snarl,

"Yu lying bitch!" and the strap came down again. Didn't she see I was dying, or already dead?

Me? Still gasping and gagging, my eyes filled with tears, I sank lower down to a crawling position. But instead of crawling, I curled against the floor and wall. The lashes kept raining down on my body, while momma cursed, "Dirty...little...bitch...tell lie...pon...me...man...Slut...whore...stooge...."

I was sure I was going to die.

When my breathing was sufficiently improved, I began to scream for murder. But momma didn't stop until she was exhausted. By then my body was a mass of criss-crossed welts.

Needless to say, she was convinced that I had lied about daddy being my lover. Even now I just cannot understand why she didn't believe me.

I am sure momma didn't ever tell daddy, or anybody else, that I had told her he had been my first lover. As she had said after flogging me, she was totally sure I had lied because I had inherited my real father's vices – lying and whoring. I am sure that she had never had even a moment's doubt about her husband's 'upright-fatherly' manner towards me, convinced her precious husband would never have so much as thought of having sex with me. I never repeated the fact to her, didn't try to explain, and thereafter our mother-daughter relationship became less binding than before – though we didn't stop loving each other. She was the type of woman who could never hate her child, and I surely couldn't hate her for what she did. In fact, within an hour after that unforgettable flogging I felt, and still do, that the abuse had cleansed me of the sin I had committed against her and her marriage. Still, I was very dismayed that she should have thought me capable of telling such a lie against her husband.

But looking back now, I am forced to think that perhaps her disbelieving me was really one of the best things she ever did. Events that followed years after made it seem possible that if she had believed me she and I wouldn't be as happy as we now are, almost fifteen years later.

46

Momma and daddy had caught Kevin and me making love on a Wednesday night. For two days I didn't so much as go near our mesh-wire gate and bamboo fence. And I was glad Kevin kept out of sight. By the time I saw him on Saturday, most of my welts had disappeared and the scabs were almost dried up. And daddy had apologized for beating me.

As soon as he had arrived home Thursday evening, daddy came to my room. "Forgive me fo' beating yu," he whispered soothingly. "Yu know I love yu." His face was sombre – I was lying in bed, glaring at him with open contempt; momma and the boys were outside. "Is because a love yu," he whispered conspiratorily, "why a not going to tell anyone what happen. An' a tell yu mother she musn't even tell her sisters." He was leaning over me.

"I don't care what yu do," I said icily. "Never again will yu get my pussy."

"Take it easy," he coaxed, straightening to his full height, palms held out beseechingly, ears cocked and a wary look on his stubby face – obviously he had been too upset to have shaved that morning – that showed me he was scared someone might have overheard my cold avowal. Then backing away solemnly, hands still in a soothing pose, a silly smile on his face, he said, "We'll talk. Tek' it easy fo' now."

He left the room.

Next day he apologized twice, and I ignored him.

Outside of our home, only Kevin's aunt and her husband knew that Kevin and I had been caught making love; my brothers knew something was amiss but didn't know what had happened, they had slept through it all. The family which lived two chains below us hadn't heard my screams when daddy was flogging me, and the family that lived in front of Kevin's aunt's house was away for a few days. So because Kevin, his aunt, her husband, momma and daddy, didn't tell anybody, I was spared from being the victim of juicy gossip.

On Saturday evening, my younger brother and I were returning home with some coal we had just bought on the main road when we met Kevin near the coal-man's house. The evening was

very overcast, black clouds right across the sky. "Rainy season going to start any day now," the jet black coal-man had observed.

Kevin and I fell back behind my brother, who was carrying a box of coal on his head – I was carrying a large shopping bag with handles.

Kevin said nothing about our ill-luck and I couldn't place his facial expression. But my uneasiness didn't last for more than a few seconds, as he immediately sprang a gem. "I leaving Monday," he whispered. "Why yu don't just come with me?" (My head swelled) "I will take good care of you. I going to start work as soon as I go back."

I stopped and beamed at him, my pulse racing excitedly, feeling ten feet tall. Running away would put me of out daddy's reach, and I was sure that momma and daddy wouldn't send the police after me – this proved to be quite correct.

"My parents will like you when I explain things to them," Kevin said softly. "Plus a have somewhere else where you can stay at first."

"I love you so," I said breathlessly. Oh, how my eyes must have been dancing and glowing!

We fell further back behind my brother, who understood that Kevin and I were talking 'love secrets'. While strolling along we made our plans for leaving on Monday morning. I was so dazed by excitement, the bus and car and two bikes that passed by seemed unreal, the people we walked by were like ghosts. We parted at the top of our lane – he went back up the main road.

Walking down the lane with my brother, I felt like a queen. I trusted Kevin and our love. But if he should abandon me at some point in the future, I mused that night, I would be able to get a job in Kingston as a live-in helper. After all, though I was now only fifteen, I knew I could wash, cook, clean and iron better than most twenty-year-old girls.

Yes, running away to Kingston was the best move, I thought. I would make Kevin real happy, so happy he would go to pieces if I threatened to leave him. But I would insist that we mustn't have any babies before I was eighteen or nineteen. Ah, bliss...

Sunday night while the rest of my family slept, I packed my better items of clothing into a small card-board box, and took the $20 worth of coins and notes from by savings box. It wasn't too hard to do these tasks with the lamp turned low as if I was asleep (like most rural folks who used kerosene lamps, we didn't put out our lamps when going to bed). But I had to be silent because since catching Kevin and me making love, momma had begun to leave the door connecting the two bedrooms partially open – but she closed the floral curtain that hung on their side of the door. Thus I couldn't turn up the lamp and, with a racing heart, kept an ear cocked for sounds from momma and daddy's room.

When Kevin tugged at the cord on my big toe I was awake. It was then shortly before 4:00 a.m. I crept out the back door, after putting on my newest jumper-suit over fresh underwear. We didn't go through our gate; we crossed over into his aunt's field and went through the barbed wire fencing. I washed my hands, feet and face at the stand pipe at the top of our lane. Then I put on my white socks and my best pair of shoes. And I tied my 'china-bumped' hair in a new scarf – the china bumps, which a friend had done last evening, had held up well through my night of restless sleep; I had tied my head in a thick cloth.

Except for the numerous crows of cocks, the pre-dawn hour was still and cool and mellowed by the pale quarter moon. As Kevin and I had hoped, nobody else from down the lane came out to await the early buses. Still, we stood in the shadows a little distance from the street light near the wall at the mouth of the lane.

We didn't do much talking, hadn't since I had crept from my former home – that's how I already saw daddy's house. Neither of us mentioned the future. But from the ecstatic look on Kevin's face I was then sure we would enjoy a happy lifetime together.

How wrong I was!

We took the first of the two early morning buses. It came down the road just before the first signs of dawn showed in the east after 5:00 a.m. Fifteen minutes later we got off at the T-junction where the Belfield main road met the major road from Port Maria – the

parish capital – to Kingston. It wasn't long before a minibus bound for Kingston bore us away from that cane-field bounded road junction where the sea was only a mile away.

I was elated. Daddy couldn't use my body anymore. I was free. And momma wasn't going to see me again before I was lawfully an adult. I was going to miss her and my brothers.

Kevin and I didn't talk much on the twenty-nine mile journey to Kingston. And when we did talk they were brief observations about the journey – the driving, the road, etc. We were sitting at the back of the minibus, which became crowded by the time it had covered the first one-third of the journey. Then it was a swift non-stop drive along the clear winding road through the hills along the narrow valley cut by the Wag Water River.

This wasn't my first journey to Kingston; I had been there on two school trips. But this time my anticipation of a happy future with Kevin gave the journey a heady excitement. I was contented to sit by my love's side and observe. In the dull, early morning light the misted valleys and hills, homes, closed shops, farms and people we sped by all seemed sacred and special to my slowly roving eyes. I was a princess running away from horrors with the knight of my dreams, the man I loved who, I was sure, would take good care of me. Together, I planned, my love and I would climb to greater heights, have wonderful children and be ever happy.

I was bubbling over with ecstasy when we got off the minibus at Half-Way-Tree square. It was shortly before 8:00 a.m. The mellow morning sun was now fully up on the city. The morning traffic jams weren't on as yet. We took a J.O.S. bus down to the intersection of Hagley Park and Waltham Park roads. I did enjoy this my first ride on a city bus – called 'Jollies' – even though it was packed with early workers and school children. From there it was a short walk to our destination in the crowded ghetto of Mongoose Town – a teeming little area that was rather narrow but much longer, with unpaved zinc-lined lanes.

I knew I was going to stay with some of Kevin's friends' for a

while'. But the reality was completely different from what Kevin had led me to believe.

It turned out to be a nightmare.

Kevin didn't love me. He had brought me to Kingston to be a camp whore – for a den of gunmen.

Chapter 6

My first twenty-four hours in Mongoose Town showed me
what it was like to be really fucked. I was 'shafted' – that seems
the right word – or rather my pussy was assaulted – so often that
for days it was sore and constantly churning.

Mongoose Town was then a crowded mass of small board and
a few concrete houses, shacks, zinc fences and unpaved lanes; but
there was water and electricity. It begins on Waltham Park Road
and extends down to the Payne Land area. The people were a
rugged looking lot, and it was a Socialist strong-hold. (Kevins'
parents didn't live there, they lived a fair distance away on Waltham
Avenue.)

Our destination was a three-room board house in the middle
of the area; this unpainted board house was where the six-man,
four-girl Trigger Squad lived. There was also a three-bedroom
house in the zinc-enclosed yard which belonged to the Reids who
had ten sons aged sixteen to twenty-eight years. The three youngest
Reid boys, Kevin and two other young men made up the male section of the Trigger Squad, and they had pooled resources to build
their three-room house.

The two houses took up most of the yard, leaving only a narrow
strip of grassless land between and around the houses. There was a
pipe and modern bathroom facilities at the back of the Reid's house.

The Trigger Squad members were Kevin, Head and Ray, and
the Reid brothers Banny, sixteen, Shut, seventeen and Scaba, nineteen. The brothers were tall and black, with the very large protruding eyes that all ten Reid brothers had inherited from Mr Reid.
Head, eighteen, was short, thick and brown with a large head that
earned him his name. Ray, eighteen, was of medium height, black
and handsome. All were from Mongoose Town or nearby.

The girls were Susan, seventeen, a short plump brown com-
plexioned earth-mother; Whory, thirteen, a short, slim half-Indian;
Evan, sixteen, tall, trim and black; and Janet, eighteen, slim, black

and of medium height. Whory had run away from her home in St Ann; she was the only one who wasn't from Kingston. Like the boys they rarely talked about their past.

The Squad was asleep when Kevin and I arrived. One of their three rooms was furnished with a five-piece dining set and a worn sofa. In each of the other rooms were three mattresses covering most of the floor. Immediately I realized that Kevin and his friends were gunmen – I saw guns. (Mr Reid and all his sons were thieves and gunmen.)

Fear gripped me. Suppose the police were to come now...a shoot-out, and I would be killed! Why did I run away with Kevin?

Kevin saw me staring at the guns and must have seen my thought reflected on my face. "Don't worry," he said nonchalantly. "We safe. Fi we party rule."

That didn't ease my fear, especially because his eyes and voice seemed to have changed. However, it wasn't long before I was forced to put aside such thoughts by the frequent sexual assaults by Kevin's love colleagues and three of the older Reid brothers who still lived at their parents' house.

I knew it was senseless to plead or protest. They terrified me without saying one harsh word – they were mean-looking gents – so I did my best to please them. I pretended that I was a prostitute on the job. Perhaps I shouldn't have given them my best, because they all declared how good I was and for the next twenty-four hours each kept returning for more.

For several days I was constantly watched and tactfully confined to the yard. Hatred for them all filled me. I only spoke when questioned, and did my best to avoid having sex with Kevin. I wanted to run away, but didn't get any chance to do so.

Then they began to allow me to move about in the area with the girls, who I know were under orders to keep a close watch on me. By the end of my second week there, I began to give in, I no longer thought about returning to the country. Instead, I began to think of looking for a job as a live-in helper somewhere in the city.

Both the boys and the girls were kind and loving to me. But

still I was bitter with Kevin; I had not come to Kingston to be a camp whore.

At least one night each week, some or all of the boys went out on robbery sprees, sometimes taking two or three of the girls for carrying the guns and/or loot. On such a night three weeks after my arrival, all six boys, Susan and Whory went out. The two other girls and I sat in the sitting-dining room watching the television that the boys had recently stolen.

"Carlene," Janet said kindly in her coarse tone, "I know Kevin didn't tell yu the truth 'bout what him was taking yu into. But yu have to agree them treat us good, an' one day them going to rob a bank an' all a us will be rich." She sipped her beer, I took a gulp of mine.

"Yea," Evan intoned; "plus yu did want to leave home."

"I am okay," I said evenly. "I just don't like living like a prisoner."

"The boys 'fraid that yu want to go back home," Janet said solemnly, gazing at me steadily, her black face stoical. "Them like yu, an' we girls like yu too. We all want yu to stay."

"They soon allow yu to go shopping with us," Evan assured, "an' to dances an' clubs. Jus' keep taking yu pills so yu don't get pregnant."

They were both gazing at me, expecting a reply. The beer had given me a cozy feeling. I sighed. One the debators on the television screamed some silly nonsense: their debate didn't interest us.

"A jus' don't like being shared by a group of men." I spoke in an even tone. "But I really don't want to go back to the country. Why can't each of the boys just stick to one girl…"

"Oh Carlene," Evan groaned; "Young girls like us who poor musn't talk 'bout love or one man an' baby. We must aim to better we-self while having fun with the boys we like. Then when we start have children it will be easier to be faithful to our husbands."

"Money," Janet said passionately, "is wha' we must look 'bout. That is ambition!"

Just then an interesting movie began, and we fell silent. But I

54

wasn't following the movie. I sat gulping my beer and musing on the last two statements the girls had made. And the more I thought the more sensible these statements seemed: wisdom not taught in school, knowledge gained via common-sense on the viciously colourful streets of the ghetto. And didn't the Trigger Squad girls seem happier and more beautiful than the young mothers in the area who had a special lover? My thoughts and the beers gave me a special high. Yes, the girls were wise.

But I was still uneasy about living outside the law. Would I dare transport guns or loot?

Because the three eldest Reid brothers, who didn't live with their parents, were the 'dons' in the area, the Trigger Squad was not only feared but was also much loved by all of Mongoose Town, and we girls were treated respectfully by all. Except for the older Reid boys, no man outside of the Squad approached us sexually. All members of the Squad, including myself, received a weekly cheque under the government's 'Crash Programme' project without doing any work: those persons who worked didn't begrudge us because it was thanks to men like the Reid brothers and the boys of our Squad that gunmen from other areas didn't terrorize Mongoose Town.

By my fourth week I was broken in completely. I had long ago dismissed all thought of returning to the country, and, since my talk with Janet and Evan, I was becoming more and more displeased with the idea of becoming a household helper. In short, I was enjoying my easy life with the Squad. So I thought it was time for them to allow me to venture outside of Mongoose Town, seeing that I was getting a weekly salary plus pocket money from the boys. I especially wanted to go shopping with the girls.

On my fourth Friday morning with the Squad, we had an early breakfast. Then we girls washed the dirty dishes and tidied the house. Next we sat down with the boys in the sitting/dining room. Everyone was in a good mood, looking forward to mid-day when we would go collect our 'Crash Programme' cheques from

the oldest of the Reid brothers: he always changed my cheque but the others usually went to the bank just for the fun of going.

I had not told Kevin that my stepdaddy and I had been lovers. Now I intended to tell the Squad an edited version, as a show of goodwill for them.

"I want yu all to stop treating me like a prisoner," I announced nervously, after having gained their full attention. I paused and my eyes roamed over the boys. Silence, thick, heady. I took a deep breath and plunged ahead: "I don't want to go back to the country, because my step-father was always trying to rape me." I forced a smile to cover my shame. "I want to stay here."

They all beamed like delighted ten-year-olds. Kevin's and my eyes met, and for the first time since my arrival I smiled at him.

"I did know yu would like our set-up here," he said happily.

"This call fo' a celebration tonight," Ray said sweetly. "Mek' we go to the dance over Jungle."

That night I went to my first dance. Next morning when we returned I was drunk and happy.

I began to go shopping with the girls. Weekend nights we went to clubs and dances. And on Wednesday afternoons, we went to the movies.

By the eighth week with the Squad I was drinking, smoking (marijuana and cigarettes) and cursing as much as the other girls. And I was learning a lot about people by being observant wherever I went; I was especially fascinated with the male characteristics. A city can teach so much if one is observant and spends time to listen to the numerous sounds and voices. Yes, I was enjoying myself, and the boys didn't involve me in their robbery schemes.

Since I had decided to stay with the Squad – at least for a few years – I was once again on good terms with Kevin, and was grateful to him for bringing me to Kingston: it even amused me to think that I had once thought I was in love with him. Like the rest of the Squad – boys and girls alike – I was now of the opinion that love and babies were for financially comfortable people: plus I had little regard for the so-called joys of motherhood.

If I had not come to Kingston with Kevin, I reflected, I would have been back home allowing my stepdaddy to use my body or fighting a running battle to keep him from doing so. Would I have been able to keep him from fucking me? It surely wouldn't have been much of an effort for him to rape me when momma wasn't home: I was too weak for such a strong man. Complaining to momma would have been out of the question. And to complain to somebody else (or scream when he cornered me) would have made me a public spectacle, which I would have preferred to avoid and allow him to fuck me.

Yes, I was sure, life with the Trigger Squad was better than what it would have been if I had remained in Belfield. And it was best that a girl shouldn't trust any one man, especially if he was poor. Why? Hadn't my father disowned me, my stepdaddy exploited my innocence, and Kevin, though I was now grateful to him, had lied to me. No, I concluded, I, of all girls, shouldn't trust men. Perhaps someday I would meet a rich man who would want me as his wife, this would be different, such a man I would trust. Money...

Still, I had no intention of staying with the Squad for more than a few years, then I would seek an office job as some form of clerk.

The Squad had two S90 motor bikes on which the boys took me to the other Socialist strongholds in the city – Concrete Jungle, Trench Town, Whitehouse, Wareika Hills, Kintyre, Superstar Corner in Hannah Town. I met all the 'Dons' for these areas and saw all forms of guns. Soon I lost my fear of guns and was willing to move about with one or two in my bag. In fact it gave me a heady feeling to pass policemen with guns in my bag, especially if I knew that the gun I was carrying was deadlier than that of the policeman.

But in February 1976, I was forced to do more than I had bargained for. Much more.

And there was the feeling that I didn't really know them. None of them, boys and girls, talked much about their past and their relatives.

Chapter 7

Armed robbery. That was what I was forced to participate in, in broad daylight, in downtown Kingston. Not far from Central police station.

Christmas 1975 had passed for me in a dazzling mixture of sex, smoking, food, drink, music and dancing. Definitely my happiest Christmas up to then. January 1976 crawled by as January always does. Political violence was now intense and there was a State of Emergency on. But we were safe in Mongoose Town. February came, and I was now in my fourth month with the Squad. And Kevin formulated a daring plan to rob one of the leading department stores on King Street in downtown Kingston.

What alarmed me was that I was expected to play a major role, which I didn't dare refuse to do. To have protested would have meant severe punishment. Possibly death.

By now I saw nothing wrong with robbing the rich, especially if the loot was insured against robbery. But taking part in an armed robbery was frightening.

Again I began to think of running away and seeking a job as a household helper. But I was unable to get away before the day planned for the robbery; they were aware of my fear and had once again begun to treat me like a prisoner.

However, on the day before the robbery, I cut a job advertisement from the *Gleaner* newspaper, with the firm intention of escaping soon after the robbery and trying to get a job. If I didn't get the job, I decided, I would return to the country. Better to be daddy's lover than to be risking my life with the Squad.

I would have been willing to carry the boys' guns to the robbery scene. Taking part in the actual robbery was just too much for me.

At 3:00 p.m. on the last Saturday in February, Scaba and I got off one of the Squad's motorbikes in front of one of the largest depart-

ment stores downtown; the licence discs that were on the bike had been stolen a few days ago. The sidewalk was crowded with hawkers and shoppers. Scaba and I were wearing dark glasses and dressed like upper class American-minded dudes – afro wigs, bell-bottom pants, leather jackets and high-heels – chattering with the Harlem accent, all 'dig', 'baby', 'sugar', etc.

Strangely enough I was relatively calm. True, I was a bit high on marijuana. But my calm state was mainly due to the fact that I had convinced myself that it was in my own interest if I did the job well. In the travelling bag on my shoulder was a sub-machine gun.

Shut, Danny, Evan and Whory were already in the store. Kevin, Head, Susan and Janet were on the sidewalk. All were armed with automatic pistols.

Kevin, Head, Susan and Janet were to remain outside, on the lookout for cops. Shut was to disarm the store detective. Danny was to rob the manager's office when Scaba and I entered the store. I was to help Scaba, the boys said, because the other girls would be of more help to the other guys in case there was shooting after Scaba and I rode away.

There were no policemen about, so Scaba and I entered the store. Danny moved towards the back of the store. Shut went to work on the store detective. Scaba took the gun from my bag and waved it. The nearer customers fell back silently.

"Money!" Scaba snarled, as I began to work my way down the bank of terrified cashiers. Two minutes later I had most of the cash in my bag. Then he and I rushed out of the store, followed closely by Shut.

At about the same time that Scaba and I rode off, Danny was escaping via a back door into the alley behind the store. (Because Scaba and I had been the centre of attraction, the others were able to get away on foot easily.)

Scaba and I rode to Wareika Hills safely. Ray was there with a borrowed Honda 360 – Scaba and I had used one of the Squad's Honda S90s. I took off my afro wig, sun-glasses and leather jacket.

Then Ray and I rode to Mongoose Town on the 360. Scaba arrived two hours later, having changed his clothes and replacing the stolen licence disc on the S90.

By 6:30 p.m. the full Squad was assembled at our H.Q. Now I was so nervous I had to be chain smoking cigarettes to keep myself from trembling. Our total haul was $60,000 – most of it had come from the Manager's office. Danny said he had found the manager counting money and had knocked him unconscious. Shut had taken the store detective's .38 revolver.

Like each girl, I was given $3,000.

Sunday night I was the only Squad member who didn't get drunk. I was planning to desert them next morning.

We had stayed home Saturday night, all of us mentally exhausted by our daring robbery. Sunday was spent quietly, restless as Sundays always were. Nobody outside the Squad, including the seven oldest Reid brothers, knew that we were the gang who had pulled off what the news described as a daring and well-planned robbery.

Then, Sunday night the Squad released its pent-up elation via a wild, drunken orgy. Of course, I only pretended to be merry and to be drinking a lot. I drank very little, but made sure the others all drank a fair amount of overproof white rum mixed with wine, fixed by me.

I awoke at 4:45 a.m. next morning and packed most of my clothes in a large travelling bag I had recently bought. The rest of the Squad were sound asleep, dead to this world. I took a bath, dressed, stuffed my $3,000 share of the loot and $200 savings down in my travelling bag and hurried away in the misty pre-dawn. The note I had left behind said:

> *Dear Squad,*
> *Thanks for your kindness. Be assured I won't*
> *ever tell anybody about you. I am not brave*
> *enough to continue with you.*
> *But I love you all,*
>
> > *Carlene.*

My pulse was racing as I hurried up the lane towards Waltham Park Road. All was quiet on the misty and dark and deserted lane. There were no street lights in the area. Knowing there would be a group of armed men on guard duty at the top, I began to sing.

"Which daughter that?" a voice challenged.

"A Squad member," I replied, moving toward them without pause. "A carrying some things to me family in the country." I was now alongside them, five of them heavily armed.

"How yu so early?" It was 5:30 a.m.

"A want to come back this evening," I replied sweetly.

"Pass through, yu safe. We se' no stinkin' labourite since we come ya."

"5:30 gone. She safe. Soon se' bus."

I passed on. Forty feet ahead was Waltham Park Road.

I was standing on Red Hills Road by Purity Bakery sniffing the wonderful aroma of bread baking. The early morning traffic was still thin – it was now 6:45 a.m.

After leaving Mongoose Town, I had walked briskly to Hagley Park Road, still afraid that the Squad might awake and come after me. Soon I got a bus to Half-Way-Tree and took a No. 37 bus as the conductress on the first bus had told me to do. Only then did I feel safe. But because it was so early I got off on Red Hills Road, where I now stood humming merrily.

At 7:45 a.m. I took another No. 37 bus up to Havendale. Now I was nervous, afraid I wouldn't get the job. Dear God, I prayed, please let me get this job so I won't have to return to my step-father's house.

The bus conductress directed me to Oldgate Drive. I took off my cheap watch: I wanted to look dirt poor.

It must have been shortly after 8:00 a.m. when I knocked at No. 80 Oldgate Drive. An overfed dog yapped a few times from the carport before a plump, brown lady came onto the verandah. Lady and dog moved slowly down the short driveway towards the gate.

I was nervous, pluse racing.

The lady was short with a handsome round, face, and looked about forty.

"Good mornin' mam," I said slowly, like a nervous country girl struggling to speak proper English, in vain. "I se' you advertisement in the *Gleaner* and come this morning from mi home in St Mary with mi clothes." My eyes were half downcast. "So if you want me I will start work today."

She regarded me closely. Like a real 'raw country girl', my eyes were half lowered, hands locked in front of me and the toes of my shoes (my worst pair) digging at the concrete.

"Suppose I don't accept you?" she asked authoritatively, squinting up into my half-lowered eyes.

"I will have to go back to the country now, mam," I said pathetically. "A don't have any family here in town." I glanced at her, my eyes begging for pity.

Silence for endless seconds. I was sweating, not because of the bright morning sun. She was as cool as a cucumber. She passed a well manicured hand over her thick black hair which was tied in a bun.

"How old are you?"

"Sixteen and a half, mam." Without pause I added rapidly, "but a can wash and cook good, mam. A will even work fo' only food. Me parents hav' six of us an' havin' it real hard. Please give me a chance, mam." My story was false, but my desperation was real This job, even only for food and shelter, would give me a chance to plan my future and I would be safe from the Squad.

I got the job. My pay was to be food, shelter and $8 per week, with Saturdays as my day off. My living quarters, at the back of the four-bedroom house, were small but comfortable – a small room with a dresser, crude wardrobe and a fairly new three-quarter bed, and a tiny bathroom.

Mr and Mrs Bell had three children – Carl, seventeen; Tony, thirteen; and Marva, eleven. The area in which they lived was a middle class one at the foot of Mannings Hills and Great House

Circle Heights where the rich lived in large mansions. Like the Bells', most of the homes in their community were bungalows.

Mrs Bell did all the cooking and some of the ironing, and insisted that the children kept their rooms tidy.

On my second day I pretended to send off a letter to my family. Would Mrs Bell notice and ask why I didn't receive any reply? Whether or not she noticed, it turned out she didn't ask anything about my family.

As soon as Mr Bell first laid eyes on me I knew he would soon begin to ask me for sex. What I didn't anticipate was that the son, Carl, would also want to fuck me, and would succeed via a callous plan.

Chapter 8

Mr Bell and I were making passionate love in a motel room on the Waterfront downtown. Through the window of our third floor room I could see the calm, glassy, blue-green Caribbean sea.

Mr Bell was a short, black, middle-aged accountant with a slightly protruding belly and a small bald spot towards the back of his low thinning head of black hair. I was giving him my best. And he was a good lover. A half-hour before I had given him what he said had been his first experience of being blown; at first he had feared I might have bitten his short, stout prick, but in the end he had been pleased. Now he was fucking me doggy fashion, my eyes on the sea, the salty taste of sperm in my half-open mouth.

It was a Saturday, the first of many Saturday meetings we were to have in this same motel. But it was our second sexual encounter.

Our first sexual engagement had taken place on my fourth Sunday with the family. Mrs Bell and the children had left for church at 7:45 a.m., the car driven by Mrs Bell. Less than five minutes later, Mr Bell came to the kitchen and without a word he began to massage my bum. I was washing dishes at the sink. I wasn't surprised, long aware of how he eyed me with desire, and I had been wondering how long he would take to begin the ball rolling.

"You are a sexy girl," he said, and pinched my bum lightly. "Be nice to me and I will be kind to you."

"How can I be nice to you?"

I had not moved, but had turned my head towards him. 'I would like yu to be kind to me." My voice was calm, slow and steady.

"Let's go to your room and I'll show you!"

"But we have to hurry," I said firmly. "I have to tidy the house before Mrs Bell returns."

We went to my room and had a passionate but quick fuck. After, as we were dressing he said: "Whoever taught you, did a good job. It is good to have a real woman in the house."

My eyebrows shot up. "What about yu wife?"

"She use to be damn great in bed, but for the past two years she just not interested anymore."

"I wish there was some way we could do it often." My tone was wistful, though purely histrionics. It seemed a good chance to get a steady flow of gifts. "But perhaps yu already have other women."

"Nobody special. Just when the chance arises." Then thoughtfully: "But perhaps you and I could arrange something special."

That was six days ago. Now here we were in a downtown motel room. He had driven away from home early that morning. I had left at 8:00 a.m. and walked to Red Hills Road, from where I took a taxi to the motel.

Now, after he had had me doggy fashion, we lay in each other's arms. "It is a good thing my wife hired you," he said contentedly. "The best thing she ever do in a long time."

"I glad yu enjoy making love with me."

"I am going to give you some money at the end of each month," he said.

My spirits soared. "If yu…you want to," (I was struggling to speak properly), "but it's not money why I make love with you. I love you."

"It is good to be loved by such a lovely young girl like you," he responded proudly. I smiled, he was now truly tied to me. "But," he added gently, "I must give you some money, I know what it is to be poor. And a young girl needs so many things."

Then he started talking about his past. He was the only child of a poor christian couple in rural St James, who had made great sacrifice to send him to high school where he had won a scholarship to college. Then he asked me, "Tell me about yourself."

I told him a pitiful story about being from a large family with gentle and hard-working parents.

He hugged me closer. "I'll take good care of you from now on. Trust me." We were silent for a while, then he said, "Seeing that you sucked my private, you might be expecting me to return the compliment? I have never tried it."

"You don't have to."
"Perhaps I will."
I began to massage his groin.

My $3,200 was well hidden in my room. Slowly I began to forget about the Squad. I knew I wouldn't meet them on the Waterfront downtown, they didn't dare set foot there because they were well known by the "Southside 'High-up' Tuffs" who controlled the Waterfront and were bitter enemies of the Squad. And the Squad didn't have any friends in or near the area where the Bells lived. Plus, I knew all the places they frequented.

At nights I would lie awake for hours wondering how to make my future financially bright. I had no intention of being a household helper for long. And I knew Mr Bell couldn't afford to support the lifestyle I desired – my own comfortable apartment, expensive clothes, jewellery, exciting night-life, etc. Plus, even if he could, why should he when he could have me for a small allowance? And it wasn't only because he was kind and a good lover why I was willing to be his paramour: there was very little doubt in my mind that had I rejected him he would have found some way to make me lose my job at their house.

I didn't think much of finding a husband, since I knew I would never marry a man if he wasn't rich. And I was wise enough to know that though most rich men would keep poor girls like me as mistresses they, except for very few, wouldn't think of marrying the likes of me. Plus, men had hurt me all my life, so, although I enjoyed sex with them, I thought I could never really be 'head-over-heels in love' with any man, rich, or poor.

Children? I didn't feel any maternal urge.

I knew I wasn't educated enough to get a well-paid job, so I thought of using my money to attend night classes. I even thought of prostitution but found the idea repulsive – not that I looked down on prostitutes; I just wasn't suited for that trade.

My final decision was shaped by the many sexy novels which the Bells owned.

Though I had not completed primary school I was a good reader. Mrs Bell gave me permission to read her novels and old magazines, and she lent me an old dictionary. The first novel I read (by Robbins) showed me what to do, thereafter I read for at least two hours every night.

My aim was to improve my speech and etiquette; cultivate alluring charms and wit and a sense of humour; improve my poise and figure; and gather an impressive wardrobe and learn how to apply make-up skilfully. Then I would seek out rich middle-aged and old men who were generous and in need of young mistresses. Surely in ten years I could gather a fortune? Perhaps go to school by day while my keepers were at work?

I studied the beauty, fashion and society pages of all newspapers and magazines which Mrs Bell bought. And I kept a close eye and ear on Mrs Bell and her many friends who came to visit her.

I soaked up information like a sponge, kept to a diet, and exercised every morning. And I kept reading those 'block-busters' novels.

Then the son, Carl, intervened.

Threatening my affair with his dad.

Chapter 9

Seventeen-year-old Carl Bell was five foot six, slim, handsome and energetic with a dark brown complexion. The sparse bumps on his face seemed to beautify rather than taint, and his afro hair-style seemed a bit too much for a high school boy. He represented his school in cricket and football, and was popular at school – a steady flow of male and female school-mates were always in and out of the house.

During my first month there, he and I only exchanged daily greetings. Of course I addressed him as Mr Carl, while he called me Carlene. I didn't notice him showing any sexual interest in me, but, as events would prove, he must have had his eye on me.

I was dismayed when he began to show an interest in me, or rather my body. Young men, especially teenagers, had no place in my plans, and I didn't like the idea of bedding father and son. Plus I knew that if Mrs Bell suspected that her son was so much as thinking about sex with me, she would have fired me – she was the type of woman who thought that teenagers shouldn't have sex, and that all girls from a poor background were too sexual.

Whenever he wasn't in danger of being overheard, Carl began to pay me passionate compliments – "Why is there no girl at school as sexy as you?" "Carlene, you are a gem, a very rare one." "A girl like you should be a movie star."

His tongue was sweet. I responded to his compliments like a shy virgin, praying that he would soon lose interest in me. I didn't dare show him my true feeling, which was contempt. I sensed that rebuffing him wouldn't have been in my best interest.

One Friday – when I had been on the job for about two months – he stayed home from school. Throughout the morning he stayed in his room studying, preparing for his G.C.E. 'O' Level examinations. At midday Mrs Bell left in a taxi to do her weekly shopping. I was in the back-yard washing some clothes.

Shortly after his mother had left, Carl came into the back yard.

"Princess, you are hard at work." His charm was on full blast. "A beauty like you shouldn't work so hard. If I was good at washing I would help."

I didn't so much as glance at him. I was standing, my hands busy in the concrete wash tub which was built onto the wall. "I am glad for the job, sir," I said nonchalantly.

"Don't 'sir' me when we are alone." He was leaning on the wall nearby. "You and I are the same age, and I love you."

I sighed exasperatedly. "Mr Carl, you momma would be angry if she heard you talking like this. Probably she would even fire me."

"I won't endanger your job. I am in love with you."

"Mr Carl…"

"Stop calling me Mr when we are alone. I love you. Not just lust, a real need."

"I am only a helper." I glanced at him, my eyes begging him to leave me alone.

"So what? I would marry you." His eyes seemed aglow with sincerity; but I knew the damn boy had developed the male art of sensual deceit at an early age.

"Even if what you say is true, I already have a boyfriend in the country. And what about all them girls who visit yu… you, and who you go out with?"

'The girls I move with are school friends, nothing serious. And your boyfriend doesn't own you until he marries you – until which time I will do my best to make you mine."

I remained silent, eyes on my work. I could feel his gaze fixed on me. A minute later, as I began to put the sheets I had just washed into a plastic tub to carry them to the nearby lines to hang them to dry, he said: "Carlene, I am going to come out of the house tonight and spend the night with you."

"No!" I was angry, couldn't he stick to his many school girls?

"If you do I won't open my door to let yu… you into my room."

"Yes, you will," he responded with a sly grin. "If you don't I will find some way to make you lose your job, soon."

I gaped at him. Then indignation flooded my being, but I was

able to mask it when I said: "To think yu just say how yu…you love me." Our eyes were locked.

"I do." He reached out and held my water-soaked hand. I was transfixed and frightened by what I saw in his eyes, although I didn't know if it was pure cruelty, mockery, love or a mixture of all three. "I can't be in the same house and not spend a few nights with you," he continued softly. "Believe me, if you force me to make you lose your job, or if you leave, then later on in life I will find and marry you."

The brief spell under which his eyes had held me was broken. Fury filled me. I glared at him. You beast, I thought, you think I am such a fool to swallow your absurd avowal. Without a word I picked up the plastic tub of washed sheets and walked towards the clothes lines. He didn't follow.

Like all men, I thought, he was cruel. Should I give in to him or tell his father? No use telling the mother.

What should I do? If I gave in to his request, how often would he want to visit my room at nights? And what if his parents should hear him moving about one night? I had to try to hold onto my job for a while. What would Mr Bell do if I complained to him?

These questions kept returnig to my mind over and over during the rest of the day. Men were always saying they loved me when in truth they saw me only as a body, a cunt. But someday, I mused, I will be able to sleep only with those I chose – though they are all beasts I loved sex – and perhaps I might be able to get even with those who had hurt me…Daddy…Kevin and the Squad…and Carl.

By the time I returned to my room at 7:30 p.m., I had decided to give in to Carl's unwelcome demand, and prayed that his parents wouldn't find out.

I was awake when he knocked at my door shortly before midnight. I let him in and without a word or looking at him, I undressed and lay on my back with my legs spread and eyes closed. The outside lights at the back of the house spilled a bit of

light through the semi-closed curtainless glass-louvre windows, making the room semi-dark. Although I was on the pill I made him use the condom he had carried. That would rob him, I thought, of the real sweetness of my cunt.

I gave him a dead fuck, lying almost as stiff as a log while he laboured, hoping it would discourage him – as I had suspected he was no virgin who would enjoy a dead fuck. He took fairly long to climax, and before he left he warned me, "Next time a come move your waistline or else I shall carry out my threat."

I wanted to tell him how much I despised him, but when next he came, two nights later, I gave him a fairly lively fuck and he didn't last as long as the first time. And strangely, to my dismay, as it was to be whenever he fucked me, to keep myself from enjoying the act I had to keep reminding myself that I hated him. I was confused by this near betrayal by my body, and after each act I pushed this confusing fact to the back of my mind.

So Carl was coming at least two nights each week while I was spending most Saturdays with Mr Bell in the motel on the Waterfront.

In front of the rest of the family I was calm and respectful to Carl. But when he came to my room at nights my silence – in response to his absurd avowals of love – and my eyes showed him how much I despised him.

"Someday," he kept saying, "you will realize I truly love you."

Acting on Mr Bell's advice I asked Mrs Bell for, and got, the first weekend in May off to go visit my family in the country. But I didn't go to the country. Instead I checked into the Seaview Motel at 5:45 p.m. on Friday evening, for the weekend. By now Mr Bell and I were well known by the motel's small staff – the overweight middle-aged couple who owned and managed it were the type who never saw anything bad about customers if they were profitable.

Mr Bell arrived at 8:30 p.m. and left after midnight. He returned at 9:00 a.m. next morning and stayed until 3:00 p.m. Then shortly after 7:00 p.m. he was back and stayed until 2:00 a.m. Next day, Sunday, he was with me from 10:00 a.m. until 3:30 p.m. Then he

71

took me to the nearest market where I bought green and ripe bananas, which I would give to Mrs Bell as a gift from my parents. I took a bus from downtown and arrived at the Bell's home at 6:00 p.m.

It had been a hectic weekend for my cunt, but Mr Bell gave me a fair reward of money, which I added to my savings hidden in my room (except for buying underwear and an occasional dress, stockings and shoes, and make-up, I saved all my money – the $3,200 I had earned with the Squad was untouched).

For my sixteenth birthday Mr Bell gave me a gold watch.

I got another weekend off in September but told Mr Bell I was going to the country. Instead I spent Friday night at the Seaview Motel by myself and returned to the Bell's Saturday evening with ripe bananas I had bought downtown. I had lied to Mr Bell because I didn't want him to know I was a 'runaway girl'. And we did get to spend quite a few weekends together before I had to give up my job.

I spent Christmas '76 with the Bells, and ate so much I put on five pounds. From Mr Bell I received a pair of gold earrings – secretly of course – and when my birthday came in May '77 he gave me a thin gold chain (of course, I only wore his gifts at the motel). Two weeks later, Mrs Bell went to help one of her friends select a cottage on the North Coast: it was on a Sunday, and in the evening she phoned to say they had car trouble and would be spending the night at a motel. At dusk Mr Bell told me he would be coming to visit me after the children went to bed.

It wasn't until I turned off my light at 9:00 p.m. and lay down – after having read a fashion magazine – that I thought it was almost certain Carl would visit me that night. I considered going to tell Mr Bell I was sick, but knew that if I did he would still look in on me sometime in the night. It also occurred to me that Carl, and possibly the other two children, would be suspicious.

No, it was too late to do anything – or so it seemed to me – but pray that father and son wouldn't meet in my room.

Chapter 10

"Open the fuckin' door!" His voice was low and angry. I was trying to get rid of him but he was determined to enter and lay me.

Since it had occurred to me that father and son might meet in my room, I was a bundle of nerves. It was near full moon, the bright moonlight filtered through the curtain-less, half-open glass louvre windows casting eerie streaks of light across my room to where I had been lying awake on my bed – for what seemed like years – ears cocked, pulse racing and silently praying that my two lovers would come at well-spaced intervals. Then, shortly after 11:00 p.m. I had heard a knock on my door. My body stiffened. 'If it is Carl,' I thought, 'I will pretend I am sleeping and see if he might leave.' (My light and the outside lights were off; the only light was from the moon.)

A louder knock. I lay still.

The knocker forced the louvres wide open.

"Carlene. Carlene." It was Carl. I lay quiet, eyes closed. He called louder, and I knew he wasn't about to give up easily. Soon he would have the whole friggin'-fuck-cloth neighbourhood awake!

I got up, as if I had been asleep, and went to the window. "A feeling sick."

"Whay wrong?" He was suspicious.

"Me period," I groaned, "an' gripe."

"Since when woman started to see their period every two weeks?" He was angry. Who would've expected him to remember.

"Carl," I moaned, "me belly hurting me bad."

And that was when he used his first 'curse-word' to me.

"Open the fuckin' door!" he now repeated before I could've responded. It was clear he wasn't going to leave without sex.

I opened the door, quickly got out of my nightgown – I had on

73

no underwear – and began to undress him speedily. I am sure he found my eagerness odd, but he didn't say anything. As usual, he had a condom. I gave him my best performance. He didn't last long.

"It seems as if," he said contentedly, "you do best when sick. Perhaps I should stay the night."

"Please leave now." I pushed him off me and got up. "Yu…You promise we would only do it one time a night, and that you would leave as soon as you finish."

"Yeah, I don't intend to break my promise; plus I have no more boots." He got out of bed and struggled into his clothes: he looked so manly in the semi-dark, no traces of his schoolboy looks.

I was praying that Mr Bell would stay away for at least another fifteen minutes so I could take a quick shower.

"Okay, my strange love," Carl said gaily, and opened the door – to face his father.

Father and son gaped at each other, rooted for several endless seconds. I shrank to the size of an ant – the smallest type.

"I…a…er…heard…sounds and came to look," Mr Bell stuttered. He wouldn't have fooled a four-year-old. And Carl was no fool. He turned and gave me a burning glance, then moved past his father without a word.

For several fluttering seconds, Mr Bell and I regarded each other like two lost souls, both dumb and frozen. No, he didn't look angry: he looked like a brave young man whose doctor had just told him he had about a month to live.

I guess I must have looked like a lifeless article, since that was how I felt. Mr Bell opened his mouth but no sound came forth. Next moment he turned and hurried after his son.

I was rooted for several seconds suspended, mind blank. Then a puff of cool breeze rushed into the room and caressed my naked body. I closed the door, turned on the light, put on my nightgown and lay down on the untidy bed. I fought to keep my mind blank, but the thoughts came. What would happen? Should I begin to

pack my clothes? Could I have prevented father and son meeting at my door? Yes. How?...No, if I had tried to tell either one of them not to visit me, he would've been suspicious. Perhaps if I had allowed Carl inside at his first knock, I won-dered, he would've left before his father came. But what the hell...it was fate, that's what, fate.

About an hour after he had left, Mr Bell returned to my open window and called softly. I was awake, my overhead light still on.

I let him in. We sat on the bed, not looking at each other.

"How long since you and my son been lovers?" His voice wasn't angry, he sounded weary.

I told him the truth, and explained how Carl had blackmailed me into giving him sex.

"I believe you," he said simply, "and I can't condemn you for giving in to him – though I don't think he could have carried out his threat."

He shrugged carelessly. "I told him to stay away from you. Don't allow him inside again."

"Yu think him suspect us." I was sure Carl now knew all, but I wanted Mr Bell's opinion.

"Perhaps. But he won't tell his mother."

"I hope so, I don't want to have to leave here and you," I said with more sadness than the prospect really caused. I didn't want to leave there just yet, but if I had to I was confident I could find another man and job quickly.

He hugged me. "Don't worry," he coaxed. "Carl is a man, and have a whole string of horny school girls." We kissed, slow and easy. "You know," he chuckled proudly, "I am proud of my boy. Him have good taste in girls. But give him no more of your sweet self." He pushed me onto my back.

"Let me go take a shower!"

"Why?" he chuckled. "Is my seed just leave here."

"You know I always make him use condoms."

He laughed and kissed my legs.

As I had expected, Carl came by the next night. (Mrs Bell was home so there was no chance of Mr Bell coming.) I let him inside because I was scared that if I didn't he would tell his mother about his father and me. Though my room was semi-dark, I saw the mean scowl on his face.

"How long you and dad been carrying on?"

The expected question, but I wasn't sure what answer was best. So I remained silent, eyes downcast. After a few moments he said evenly, "It doesn't really matter, and I know you and dad will continue to meet on Saturdays."

I gaped at him, legs weak. I sank down onto the bed. He sat beside me. "After last night," he said, "it was obvious. Anyway dad can't come when mom is home.

"I love you but won't be able to tell you what to do with your body until I marry you."

Indignation brought me back to life. I hated when he talked about marrying me.

"What protection you and dad use?"

Before I could stop myself, I told him the truth. From then on he stopped using condoms, and began to have me twice whenever he came.

I reassured Mr Bell that Carl had stopped visiting me.

In September it all ended.

Chapter 11

Mr Bell came to my door at dawn on a Tuesday morning. I was awake but still in bed – most likely Mrs Bell was still asleep.

It was just after 5:00 a.m.

A firm knock then, "Carlene!"

I was instantly alarmed. I recognized the voice.

Knock, "Carlene!"

I jumped out of bed without responding, my pulse racing, thoughts a muddle of frightening flashes.

"Carlene." His voice was low and urgent. I opened the door. He was in pyjamas and a bathrobe, and I couldn't help thinking that he resembled something the cats had dragged out – his eyes were puffy and ringed by dark circles and there were scratch marks all over his face and neck.

"A come to warn you. Somebody saw us leaving the motel Saturday evening and tell my wife." He shrugged regretfully. "We had an almost silent fight last night. I didn't want to hurt her." He shrugged again. "Anyway, I am the one who she is mad at. She agrees to let you stay until the end of the month. So you have two weeks to find another job. I will give you a letter of recommendation." He left, leaving me rooted.

Be calm, Carlene I told myself, you have two weeks to seek a job, and you have several thousand dollars. But, of course, I was afraid to face Mrs Bell.

When we met in the kitchen an hour later, Mrs Bell seemed unruffled. (Obviously, guilt had made Mr Bell accept her attack without retaliation.) I cowered silently. What was her plan? Shouldn't she at least be scowling at me? Silent rivers run deep...Was she planning to poison me? Stab me in the back?

I was terrified, and had to use all my will power to keep from trembling.

After Mr Bell and the children left, Mrs Bell ordered me – in a calm manner – to join her at the kitchen table which was used for breakfast.

I sat down facing her, eyes downcast.

"I know that my husband came to see you at dawn this morning." Her voice was calm. "I won't bother to ask about you and my husband's affair. But I will say I am greatly disappointed in you. I thought highly of you because of your interest in reading my books and magazines.

"Now, you can stay until the end of the month and try to find another job. That's two weeks. And take my advice – stop seeing my husband and keep away from all married men, especially those who are old enough to be your father. They will give you little gifts and feed you great promises, but their intention is to use your young body. That's all I have to say."

Carl came to my room that night, I turned on the light and told him what had happened.

"You and dad should've been more careful." His voice was low and harsh.

I shrugged indifferently.

"I am going to miss you." He sounded sincerely wistful.

Sure, I thought, you are going to miss my pussy, especially seeing that your mother will most likely employ a middle-aged helper.

After a while he said, "You must let me know where you'll be when you leave here."

"Why should I?"

"Because I love you and..."

"Wrong," I interrupted indignantly. "You love my pussy. But that's over."

He sighed. "No use trying to tell you I do love you, but someday you'll know." Our eyes were locked. His expression seemed like that of a wounded and trapped animal, or such as one sees in the eyes of a dying old dog. I was tempted to reach out and draw him to my bosom. Instead I forced my eyes away, perplexed by my feelings. If he had only touched me I would've flung myself at him. Then his voice broke the spell.

"Please, before you leave, make me know where you'll be."

"So you can come blackmail me?" My tone was cold, but not as cold as I had intended it to be.

He got to his feet and shuffled away. At the door he turned as if to speak, but left silently.

My heart lurched, Why did I feel empty, as if I had just lost someone special? I despised him, yet there I was acting as if I would miss him...How could that be?

I was bewildered, so I turned off the light and forced myself to think about looking for a job.

Next morning Mr Bell came to my door. He gave me an envelope. He didn't say a word. Then he was gone. Clearly he had no intention of continuing our affair.

His manner wounded me profoundly. He is worse than his son, I though fighting back tears.

Inside the envelope was a letter of recommendation and $200.

On Friday, I saw an advertisement in the newspaper asking for a 'young girl from the country'. The address given was near to the Bell's home. Next day, in the later afternoon, I walked the one-mile journey to Waterdale Avenue.

Waterdale Avenue is a short dead-end street at the very foot of Great House Circle Heights. My destination, number 20, was a smart looking white bungalow with a hibiscus fence and a small swimming pool in the front yard. There was no back fence, the back yard ended on a steep and rocky hillside at the top of which was an imposing mansion.

A large Alsatian bitch rushed to the gate growling. I stood back and called. A tall, slim, graceful mulatto lady came outside and called the dog and told me to enter.

I walked up the driveway praying she would employ me.

Chapter 12

When I was near her I realized that Mrs Douglas wasn't really very tall. She was just a bit above average height. It was her erect model-like poise that had made her seem so tall from the gate.

"Good afternoon, mam," I stuttered politely, eyes correctly half downcast.

"Good afternoon," she responded sweetly, smiling, her eyes roaming over me from head to toe. "I am Mrs Douglas. What's your name?"

"Carlene – Carlene Clark."

"Sit down, let's talk." Gracefully she lowered her trim body onto one of the six iron-framed, light brown cushioned arm chairs which, along with four iron ash-tray tables, furnished the verandah. The dog lay down at her lovely slippered feet.

I sat down in the chair facing hers.

"So you need a job." It was a statement pleasantly said.

I glanced at her handsome, roundish face with its large eyes. "Yes, mam."

"Mmm, you don't look or sound as if you are just up from the country." Her penciled eyebrows were arched dramatically, but her mulatto face still showed kindness.

"No, mam," I responded nervously. "I have been working on Oldgate Drive since February last year." I gave her Mrs Bell's letter of recommendation, which said I was a good and honest worker but they didn't need a helper anymore.

I took a good look at Mrs Douglas while she read. She looked thirty, but I would soon learn she was thirty-four. Her thick black hair was shoulder length and looked vibrant. Her nails were long, well-shaped and expertly lacquered. She was a well-groomed lady.

After reading the brief letter she said politely, "I am going to phone Mrs Bell and ask her a few questions." She went inside.

'Oh God,' I prayed, 'please let Mrs Bell say nothing bad about me. I want, need this job. This lady is so nice and I could easily learn so much from her.'

I was gripped by fear. Mrs Bell had promised me a good recommendation if Mrs Douglas phoned her. Would she keep her
word?...Perhaps she hadn't meant to help me, had lied so as to
make me hopeful, then...After all why should she help me? Her
reaction up to now had been totally contrary to what one would've
expected.

Mrs Douglas was on the phone in the living room; I couldn't
hear exactly what she was saying because a radio was on. The call
must have lasted less than five minutes but it seemed an hour.

She was smiling brightly when she returned. "You can have
the job. You are perfect, just right. Mrs Bell said you can come on
Monday."

"Thank you very much, mam," I beamed, feeling on top of the
world. God bless Mrs Bell, I thought.

"I am glad you already have experience and your speech is fine.
You will find that my husband and I will treat you like a companion instead of a servant. We don't have any children and don't
want to adopt.

"You will be living inside the house. We have no servant's quarters. I have a day's worker who comes to wash two days per week,
and I love to cook. Your job," (by now I was glowing with pleasure), "will be to clean, tidy the house, wash dishes and help entertain guests. And, yes, the day's worker does the heavy ironing,
you will do the rest.

"I hope you won't turn out to be a prim young lady. I expect
you to make me laugh when we are alone. And you must forgive
me if at times I get very motherly."

I was elated, but was also a bit bewildered. The job and con-
ditions seemed much too alluring. What would the reality be like?

And there was something odd about Mrs Douglas' manner
which I just couldn't pinpoint, couldn't say what was amiss – I only
had this vague feeling that I was failing to grasp some obvious fact
of importance. However, by the time I returned to the Bells' home
I had dismissed my suspicious bewilderment. I needed a job
urgently, and the Douglases were offering me one on very generous terms. Why shouldn't they be generous? Weren't there still a
lot of kind people around?

I spent Saturday evening in my room, after expressing my sincere thanks to Mrs Bell. "I am glad you found somewhere quickly," she had said evenly. "Just take the advice I gave you." She paused and her eyes got hard, then: "You will be nearby, but don't you dare try to see my husband again, or allow him to convince you to resume the affair. I assure you, I can be real mean."

By now I was trembling, suddenly I was afraid of her. "I will…I am going to do as you say, mam." My voice was shaky. She turned away. I fled.

In the night I had expected Carl to visit me but he didn't. The next day passed swiftly. I didn't see Mr Bell all day and I didn't speak with Carl. It didn't take me long to pack my belongings in my travelling bag and a small box that night. I went to bed bubbling with excitement, but before I fell asleep Carl came in to my mind.

I had a strong feeling he already knew where I would be when I left next day. If he didn't know yet he could soon find out, I mused, or he wasn't the Carl I knew. Would he try to see me at the Douglases? Come to ask for me? No, he wouldn't dare, not after…Why did the thought that he might be bold enough to come ask for me, confuse me so? As if I wasn't afraid that he would blackmail me, but afraid that I would welcome him?

"Stop being stupid," I whispered desperately, "Carl is my greatest enemy. I don't ever want to see him again."

Carl and the other children and Mr Bell had already left home when I left in a taxi at 8:30 a.m. next morning. I could easily have walked the mile, but why should I when I had $4,200 in my savings box? It was a golden morning, a cloudless, sapphire-blue sky, a soft, steady breeze lessening the effect of the brilliant sunshine.

Mrs Douglas was on the verandah when I arrived. In skin tight jeans and T-shirt she looked even better groomed than when I had first seen her. At once, and ceremoniously, she led me to the room I was to occupy.

It was the type of room I had been dreaming of for years; but certainly not the type I would've expected from even a generous

employer. The pale yellow and white floral wall paper was in excellent condition. The grey floor tiles were obviously first class quality. The blue lace curtains at the windows matched the bed linen and pillow cases. The double-sized bed had a carved head-board, and there was a thick rug on the floor by the bed. The rest of the furnishings were a small chest of drawers, a dresser and stool and a bedside table with a lovely lamp. The built-in wall wardrobe had a full length mirror.

For several seconds I just stood in the doorway allowing my eyes to feast on the beauty of the room, especially the dark-stained wood surfaces. Then my eyes met Mrs Douglas' and I was sure I saw sexual desire there. But I forced the observation aside.

"It's a lovely room," I said hastily. "I hope I won't disappoint you."

"You won't." Her voice was soothing. "You also have your own bathroom." She pointed to the door.

I put down my bag and went to the bathroom, wondering why I was given such comfortable quarters. The bathroom was all pink and yellow. I felt like a princess.

If Mrs Douglas was bisexual, I thought, would I sleep with her for the good life she was offering? I didn't like the idea of sex with a woman, but I wasn't sure how I would react if she approached me sexually. All I knew was that I was going to do my best to hold on to this job.

I returned to the bedroom. Mrs Douglas took a green uniform from the wardrobe. "This is what you will wear on special occasions," she said. "The girl who was here before you was about your size. Try it on."

I took the uniform wondering why the last girl had left. I went to the bathroom and changed into the uniform. Except for the fact that the waist was a bit too roomy, it fitted me well. I returned to the bedroom.

"It is okay," Mrs Douglas announced. "There is another the same size. I'll tell you when to wear them."

I changed and she took me on a tour of the house – two other bedrooms and two bathrooms; a living/dining room; a library

den; a large well-equipped kitchen; and a washroom. It was a richly furnished house, all done in good taste.

Next, Mrs Douglas told me to go unpack my things. While doing so, I reflected on my suspicion that Mrs Douglas was bisexual. Was that why she was being kind? Would I go to bed with her if that was the only way I could keep the job? But what of her husband, surely he would suspect? Perhaps he was one of those men I had read about who loved watching two women together and then joining them?

I had read about lesbianism and had found the idea both silly and distasteful. I wasn't very religious and sometimes doubted christianity, but making love with a woman seemed degrading and, yes, cowardly – worse than bedding a married man. What satisfaction could one woman give another in bed. Why use dildos and vibrators, when the real thing was not only abundant but also spurted a juice which warmed the heart?

Yes, some men couldn't satisfy a twelve-year-old. But there are many who are masters of their tool.

Still, when I had finished unpacking, I still wasn't sure what I would do if Mrs Douglas wanted my body. I left the room praying that my suspicion was wrong and she wasn't bisexual.

When Mr Douglas arrived in his luxury Buick at 5:30 p.m. I was in the kitchen setting the small oval table for dinner. I went tense when the Buick stopped in the front carport – there was another carport at the back where Mrs Douglas parked her Fiat 125.

"Where is she?!" Mr Douglas bellowed from the living room, scaring me.

"She's in the kitchen, love," Mrs Douglas replied gaily.

'What kind of a nut house is this?' I wondered, pulse racing. 'Perhaps they are insane? And me...'

Mr Douglas strode into the kitchen. His wife close behind.

"Ah! My love she is as lovely as you said." Then he had me by the shoulders and was kissing my cheek.

I blushed and trembled slightly. Holding me at arm's length he said heartily, "Carlene don't blush." He had an American accent.

"In this house you are not just a servant to order about."

Why was I scared? He certainly didn't look insane. I forced a smile. "Good evening, sir." My voice was small, but then, his size, bearing and voice were so overwhelming and powerful. He was over six feet, muscular, hands as large as paddles, size twelve feet and jet black. His face was made pleasant by gold-framed glasses, and he looked a bit younger than his thirty-seven years. He resembled a military man more than the successful businessman he was.

But why did the obvious fact that he found me desirable scare me instead of exciting me?

We sat down to dinner at 6:00; I was to dine with them except for when they had guests. They talked and laughed while we ate – Mr Douglas did most of the talking. I smiled at his jokes and began to relax, forcing myself not to speculate on what they/he/she would demand of me.

Mr and Mrs Douglas had met in New York when she had visited an aunt in 1961. Love at first sight. Two weeks later they were married. He was from a wealthy New York family, but had always yearned for a land without cold winters. Thus he had been happy to migrate to Jamaica two weeks after marriage. He had brought his inheritance and invested it in business.

Mrs Douglas was from a distinguished family on Jamaica's north coast. Her father was a black doctor, her mother a white heiress. The family had been pleased with her choice of husband, but insisted that a large wedding feast be held at the family mansion. Thus, the Douglases could be said to have married twice.

After dinner Mrs Douglas told me to wash the dishes. Then after washing the dishes I headed for my room. They were in the living/dining-room and told me to join them.

"I am going to take a shower," I said, then hurried to my room and took a quick shower and put on a clean dress.

By now I was sure that something 'extra' was expected of me. Common sense told me it must be a sexual service – I didn't need a diploma to see that, right? But I decided not to ponder the subject. Carlene, when the big moment comes, I told myself, you'll know what to do.

85

I went to the living/dining room. Mr and Mrs Douglas were sitting apart on the antique-styled sofa, which was part of the gold and yellow flower-patterned three-piece living-room suite. The overhead lights were off but one of the two expensive lamps, sitting on mahogany end tables, was on. The tops of the mahogany dining and coffee tables glistened in the soft light. The front door was locked and the thick yellow drapes at the windows were closed. The T.V. was on, turned down low. There was a trolley with wine bottles and glasses near Mr Douglas – he and his wife were sipping wine.

"Come, sit between us," she said sweetly.

Suddenly the thick carpet felt like mud. I sat down wondering if I was starring in one of those blue movies where the wealthy, highly-sexed couple seduces the young virgin. I felt like a virgin. A confused one. Nervous, but excited.

"Have a glass of wine," Mr Douglas said soothingly, handing me a glass. My hand shook as he poured the wine which made me think of blood, yes, from a ravished virgin cunt.

"Don't be nervous, love," he coaxed, "my wife and I are going to make you enjoy life. Teach you how to." He paused, I sipped my wine. It was good. "We are going to give you the time of your life. Won't force you to do anything against your wishes."

"Just be nice and honest," she intoned, voice cozy and velvet smooth, "and trust us."

I began to relax. Now I knew I would go to bed with them. Damn it, the life they were offering was good. Under normal circumstances I would've welcomed a hidden affair with Mr Douglas so why refuse the extras which would come from having an open affair with both of them.

Then she sealed the matter by saying, "Carlene, we haven't discussed your money." She began to caress my knee. "You can easily earn as much as $300 each week, if you are nice to us."

Our eyes met, hers were glowing with lust. Although I had decided to accept, her hand on my knee made me tense and my voice was shaky when I said, "I'll do all you want me to."

"That's my girl," he said ecstatically and hugged me. Once

again I was stiff, the contact of their body was like fire, the wine tasted like blood. I forced all thoughts from my mind and tried to concentrate on the television.

After my second glass of wine, I began to clam down, and decided not to drink anymore. I wanted to be sober when they took me to bed. Mr Douglas took a fat brown cigar from a silver cigarette case. He lit it. The strong smell of marijuana mingled with tobacco hit me – the marijuana was wrapped in specially prepared tobacco leaves. I hadn't seen or smelt marijuana since I had left the Trigger Squad.

"Have you ever smoked herbs?" he asked casually.

"No," I lied. "But I use to smoke cigarettes and my father's tobacco."

After a while he passed me the joint. (A girl on the television was about to inject herself with heroin.) I took a few puffs and passed it to Mrs Douglas.

When the joint was finished I was fairly high, but in control of all my senses. Mr Douglas began to caress my legs. She began to nibble my neck. Relax, I told myself, and treat them good, $300 per week was a lot of money.

She unbuttoned my blouse and began to kiss my breasts. His hand was now caressing my crotch. My hands were on the back of the sofa. I felt as if I was out of my body, up in the air looking down on the action. I giggled at the thought. Ecstasy began to warm me. My eyes were closed and I leaned back against the sofa's high back.

They got up and led me to their bedroom – a large, elegantly furnished, blue dominated room; the blue carpet was inches deep. In seconds all three of us were naked. Mr Douglas' erect cock was the largest I had ever seen – ten inches long and very thick, and as black as his face.

She pushed me onto my back on the king-sized bed. Then she began to eat my moist cunt. I squirmed and groaned with pleasure, while a small part of my mind protested that I shouldn't have been so ecstatic about a woman's tongue on my cunt. But she was good, using gentle fingers to open me up so her tongue could reach

inside me, nibbling my clit gently. Pleasure riddled my body. Then she positioned herself so that we were in the 69 position. She resumed eating my cunt and I just couldn't resist eating her moist, pink, sweet-smelling pussy which was now against my face.

And I loved the taste. Soon I was having a seemingly endless orgasm.

Sometime later, Mr Douglas joined us on the bed. He fucked me twice, she once. Each time he took a long time to climax. His cock felt as big as a light pole and, although his rythmn was gentle, sex with him got a bit painful in the end. He sure did need two women.

Next morning I awoke at the sound of Mr Douglas' car driving away. I glanced at the clock on one of the two mahogany night tables. 8:05. The thick blue and white floral curtains blocked out the sunlight. For a while I lay there thinking about last night. What a night it had been! True, I felt a bit ashamed, and cunt-sore, but I couldn't deny that I had enjoyed the night. I had never known such intense ecstasy before and had so many orgasms in one night – at least six.

It seemed odd that though Mr Douglas' incredible size and stamina caused some discomfort, he had steered me to more than one orgasm. And I felt confident that in time his performance would give me only pleasure – I would get accustomed to his size and stamina. The combination of his power and his wife's tenderness had been maddeningly sweet.

I got out of the bed. I was naked. My clothes were on a blue upholstered wing chair. I was about six feet from my clothes when Mrs Douglas' voice froze me, rooted me.

"Good morning, dear Carlene." Her voice was loving and her eyes gay.

Unconsciously one of my arms went across my breast and a hand flew to cover my crotch. I wanted to dive for my clothes but I was utterly rooted by embarassment over memories of the night.

"Good morning, mam." My voice was small.

She held my shoulders. "You look so lovely when you blush."

"Why you didn't wake me, mam?" I asked hastily.

"No problem, love. Did you enjoy the night?"

I blushed deeper. She giggled and kissed my cheek. "I hope you'll stay," she said, "Will you?"

"Yes," I managed to whisper. "I want to stay."

"Lovely! Most nights you'll sleep with us. Let's go take a bath." She took off her house robe.

We went into the golden bathroom, bathed each other, and romped like two school girls.

During breakfast, she told me I didn't have to worry about getting pregnant because Mr Douglas' sperm count was very, very low.

"We are glad it worked out that way," she explained, "since neither of us want children. Our sex life cut out any thought of children. But we do love children so we give a lot of money to orphanages."

She told me that she had been a bisexual since high school, and it was she who had introduced Mr Douglas to the joys bisexual women could give a man. But she said she would never have married a bisexual man. I agreed with her that the thought of two men in bed was distasteful.

Mr Douglas came home shortly before 6:00 p.m. "What did you girls do today?"

"Made love, tidied the house," Mrs Douglas replied sexily, "made love again then cooked the dinner."

"I," he announced, "am extra horny this evening. I almost raped my secretary today. You two were constantly on my mind. Tonight shall be wild!"

Like the previous night we drank wine and smoked marijuana before going to bed. But this time Mr Douglas caused me great pain.

Chapter 13

I felt as if I was being torn in two. I was dazed. Was I dreaming?

As soon as we had come to the master bedroom, Mrs Douglas had turned on the bright overhead lights and the blue shaded lamps. What was the use of fucking in the dark, Mr and Mrs Douglas told me. You sleep in the dark but fuck in light! Wasn't half the joy seeing your partner's or partners' face?

Soon we were naked, and Mrs Douglas was lying on her back on the bed. I was on my knees sucking her pink cunt. Mr Douglas was fucking me from behind. Our groans of pleasure echoed in the brightly lit room. I was bursting with ecstasy. I bit Mrs Douglas' stiff clit as I climaxed. She screamed and I knew she too was in the throes of an orgasm.

Mr Douglas withdrew his stiff rod (he knew I had climaxed) from my cunt, and I wished he had continued fucking me. I watched him putting petroleum jelly on his erect manhood as Mrs Douglas and I lay quietly in each others arms. What was that for, I wondered indifferently. Then he came and moved his wife so that she was on her back with her head almost hanging over the side of the bed.

Next he lifted me up as if I was a rag-doll, and put me to stand on the carpet so that Mrs Douglas' head was between my legs. He pushed me forward so that I bent at the waist and was eating her cunt – she gripped my thighs and raised her lips to my pussy and circled my neck with her thighs. He used his legs and feet to force my legs wide. Next he pushed his arms between my thighs and locked his large hands around the back of my waist.

I was in a clamp, unable to move any part of me except my hands.

Then I felt his massive manhood attacking my asshole.

I screamed and clawed at Mrs Douglas' legs – but I had no nails to speak of. His manhood was like a burning iron pole being

shoved up my ass. That was when I began to feel as if I was being torn in two. I swooned, gasping for breath.

He began to move back and forth. The pain doubled and I vomited between Mrs Douglas' thighs. With my face in my vomit, it seemed as if he took years before he flooded my colon with sperm.

Dazed, I began to cry and vomited again. They carried me to the bathroom and washed the vomit from my face and hair. I was limp, completely in their hands. I was beyond anger. I couldn't have resisted if they had decided to kill me. I was already dead.

Mr Douglas held me in his arms like a baby and we returned to the bedroom. Mrs Douglas changed the bed linen. He laid me down on the bed. I had stopped crying but was still listless, my mind blank.

"It's because it was the first time," she coaxed, "why it hurt so much. That's how it was with me at first." She turned me onto my belly and applied a soothing oitment to my aching asshole. I just lay there like an inert object, utterly humiliated.

"Carlene, love," he said soothingly, "I promise I won't do it often. And believe me, after a while you won't find it as painful."

As if to prove that the horrid experience had been painful only because I hadn't had my ass fucked before, they made me watch him fucking her asshole for what seemed like hours. She didn't scream, and even acted as if she enjoyed the act (he used his hands to massage her breasts and cunt). But I was sure she would've preferred living without been buggered.

While they were engaged in their performance of buggery, I had begun to regain my wits – the ointment she had put on my shredded ass was very good, soothing. No use wasting time, I mused, hating the Douglases. The comforts and money they had offered me gave them the right to special treatment. But they should've told me anal sex was involved.

Would I have agreed, I thought, to allowing Mr Douglas to bugger me? Perhaps yes, maybe no. But telling me would've been the right way. Well, now that he had buggered me and seemed as

if he would want to do so again, I would have to begin thinking about leaving.

Or, I wondered, should I stay? Perhaps it was true that after a while it wouldn't be so painful. The money they were offering could do a lot. And though I had several thousand dollars I was still too young to live by myself.

After watching the display of buggery I went to my room (walking with legs wide, each step agony). There I lay in my bed pondering about the painful humiliation I had just experienced. Before I fell asleep, I decided that I had to find some way to leave the Douglases soon. If I stayed and the act of being buggered did cease to be painful, I was sure it would never cease to be humiliating to feel a cock up my asshole.

That night I had a dream which was to recur occasionally over the years. I dreamt that I was in a canoe at sea, a clam sea on a sunny day. I was alone in the small canoe, standing with a paddle in my hand. Carl Bell was in the water begging me to allow him to come aboard. "I want you to drown," I kept screaming and whenever he tried to come aboard I would hit his hand or head with the paddle. Soon, he was badly cut and bruised. Then I lost my balance and fell over board. "I can't swim!" I managed to shout before I went under, swallowing half the ocean and thinking, 'Oh God, I am going to die while Carl shall live.'

But next moment I felt strong hands grip me. Carl's hands. He swam to the boat and pulled me aboard.

Then I awoke gasping. 'Stupid dream,' I thought, 'such a silly dream. But aren't dreams usually stupid, senseless?'

Whenever this dream recurred in the future, I always dismissed it from my mind as a silly dream of no consequence. But events would eventually prove me wrong.

Next day, walking and sitting were painful, but I wasn't bleeding. As she had done last night, Mrs Douglas used ear swabs to clean my asshole with a diluted solution of Dettol, then applied that soothing ointment she had. She changed my bed linen and

gave me breakfast and lunch in bed. And she reassured me that I would eventually get used to being buggered. I acted as if I agreed with her; I thought it best to withhold my conviction that I would always find the act to be distasteful and humiliating.

She gave me some whisky and I spent most of the day dozing on my stomach. Some of her friends came by in the early afternoon (I only heard them) but she had to serve them tea herself.

I had not seen Mr Douglas before he left for work that morning. Now in the evening he brought me roses and a pair of gold earrings, and he turned on his powerful charm for my benefit.

I thanked him for the gifts, and allowed him to kiss and fondle me and feed me dinner (yes, he spoon-fed me as if I was an invalid). But my thoughts weren't pleasant – I wanted to use a large dildo in his asshole and see if he would've enjoyed it.

I wasn't in pain, but I groaned and set my face as if I was feeling great pain. They gave me pain killers and assured me I would be much better by the next day.

"Sir," I pleaded pathetically, "I beg you not to sex my anus again."

"My dear girl," he responded soothingly, "believe me you will soon learn to enjoy it. Trust me. My wife cried the first three times. And the first time she bled more than you did last night. Now she likes it."

She smiled, "It can be fun, especially with a vibrator in your cunt."

"There are men," he coaxed, soothing my brow, "who earn their living by selling their ass every night. Plus bigger things than my cock are always coming out of your ass."

There was only one thing to do, I thought wistfully: leave the job. But I didn't intend to leave before I found another 'live-in' job; I still didn't want to return to the country before I reached eighteen and was lawfully an adult.

I was able to serve tea, dressed in my maid's uniform, when two women visited Mrs Douglas the following afternoon (walking and sitting was still a bit uncomfortable).

All the women who visited Mrs Douglas, during my stay there, were either bisexuals or straight lesbians. I was fondled and taken to bed by many of them (most of them gave me occasional gifts – money, perfumes, make-up, stockings and underwear).

Sometimes a group of us piled onto the Douglases' bed or on the thick carpet in the bedroom.

Occasionally, Mrs Douglas and friends lunched by the pool and swam – I did most of my swimming in the later afternoons while Mrs Douglas cooked dinner.

I was with the Douglases for six weeks when a tall, heavy-set, blonde bull-dyke began to try to persuade me to move in with her – her former live-in lover had left her for a man. I was tempted to go so as to get away from Mr Douglas' buggering me. (It was true that after the first five or six times being buggered wasn't very painful and he was gentle and didn't do it often; but it was still a very humiliating experience.)

The blonde bull-dyke was a hermaphrodite with a thin three-inch penis of which she was overwhelmingly proud. Her name was Jo Ann but she insisted on being called Joe. I didn't go with her because she pinched and bit too much in bed; I wasn't sure she would've wanted me for long; and didn't like the idea of being a dyke's 'wife'. Plus I preferred feminine bisexuals, like Mrs Douglas. And within two weeks Jo Ann ('Joe') found a live-in lover, who like 'Joe' was in the late twenties, so she stopped 'courting' me.

Discreetly, so the Douglases wouldn't suspect, I had been try-ing to find a job. Every Thursday was my day off and Mrs Douglas said I should at least go window shopping by myself. I used part of each day off to job hunt. Everywhere I went the work seemed too hard for the small pay; and the helper's apartment seemed horrible compared to my elegant bedroom and bathroom at the Douglases.

I was getting $200-$300 from the Douglases each week, I mused, more than most teachers and secretaries were earning. Plus gifts from their friends. Old time people used to say, 'If yu want good, yu

nose have to run.' I wanted good, meaning plenty money, so I would accept Mr Douglas' buggering for at least one year if I couldn't find another job which paid at least half what I was now earning.

It made no sense, I reasoned, to even think about going to live on my own.

I was learning a lot from Mrs Douglas – cooking; caring my body; application of make-up; hair styling; etiquette; and world history, her pet subject. And I devoured her sex manuals, novels and American fashion magazines.

I was also hoping that one of the men over thirty (I still saw little prospect in men under thirty – weren't they all misers?) who came to the Friday night orgies or the Saturday night parties at the Douglases would take me as his mistress and set me up in a nice apartment complex which had security guards. Why not? Although my function at these orgies and parties was mainly being a waitress, I did my best to charm the men who were over thirty – most were. Often one or the other would take me to bed and I gave my best (the Douglases didn't mind my bedding their friends).

Every Friday night the Douglases' closest married friends, the Taylors and the Hustons, came by and the three couples had an orgy. I, dressed in skimpy costumes, served refreshments and helped play the records. Sometimes I was drawn into one sexual act or another. These orgies were confined to the Douglases' home because the Taylors and Hustons had children. The visiting couples always brought drinks and marijuana. By 9:00 p.m. everyone, except me, was high.

The Taylors were a black couple in their late thirties. The Hustons were mulattoes in their early thirties. Mr Taylor was my favourite, a very charming man. "Carlene baby," he once said, "you are special. All three of us men have screwed you, but you still call us sir and mister. Most girls wouldn't."

"True," Mr Huston intoned. We were all in the living room. The Hustons and Taylors had arrived only a short while ago.

"I am still very young," I explained proudly, "and I respect you all a lot."

95

"The only reason," Mr Taylor added, "I haven't suggested you and I elope is that I know my wife would be hopping mad about not being able to make love with you again."

"You're damn right," Mrs Taylor said saucily. "I wouldn't miss your prick but I'd sure miss Carlene's cunt." She winked at me. She and Mrs Huston were bisexuals and came to make love with Mrs Douglas and me several afternoons each week.

The Saturday night parties were held when Mrs Douglas felt the urge for one. They were large buffet style parties with music by a disco and security guards to keep out uninvited guests – sometimes we had a poolside party. People of all ages came, mostly Mr Douglas' business associates and Mrs Douglas' bisexual friends and their families. I wore my maid's uniform but because they were buffet style parties I didn't have much to do. So I was, more often than not, able to slip away to my room with an interesting middle-aged man.

Would one of them fall in love with me, or with my sexual performance, and take me away from the Douglases, and Mr Douglas' buggering? I was overjoyed to note that none of these men, nor Mr Taylor and Mr Huston, shared Mr Douglas' love of buggering.

Chapter 14

The Douglases had various types of sex aids which we used – vibrators, dildos, ticklers and cuffs for bondage games. It was a life of supreme ecstasy, except for the buggery.

Mr and Mrs Douglas rarely went out so I was rarely left alone at the house at nights. Even during the days I was hardly left alone: Mrs Douglas loved to take me along when she went shopping, and she went to her hairdresser's only on the days when the washer woman was there to keep me company.

The year drew to a close. From Boxing Day to New Year's Eve the Douglases and I stayed at a cottage complex in Negril. I was thrilled. There I was living it up like a tourist.

Yes, I had to admit, the Douglases were really good to me. They had offered me the week off but I told them I had nowhere to go because I had run away from home and didn't want to return before I was eighteen.

"I thought it strange," Mrs Douglas had said, "that you weren't getting or writing any letters. But as you know I don't love to pry."

"Why did you run away?" Mr Douglas asked cautiously.

"My step-father kept raping me," I replied shyly. "And when I told my mother she didn't believe, and she flogged me. So when I read that the Bells wanted a helper from the country, I ran away." It wouldn't, I had reasoned, have been wise to tell them about Kevin and the Trigger Squad.

"Our home is yours," Mrs Douglas said soothingly, but I got the feeling he was pleased to know I was a run-away.

Nineteen seventy-seven ended. I had been with the Douglases for three months. In my savings box I had $6,500 – a tidy sum for a young girl. (I didn't allow the Douglases to see my savings and the jewellery Mr Bell had given me.) By now I had a full set of silver jewellery that Mr Douglas had given me – necklace, earrings, bangles, bracelet, watch and armlet. And I had bought myself some gold pieces – rings, chains and pendants, earrings and a

bracelet. I had also bought myself a few elegant dresses and shoes and handbags.

On the first Tuesday in 1978, Miss Tracy Jenning came to the house while Mrs Douglas was out. The washer had not turned up for work (she was sick), so I was alone. I had just had lunch and was in the living room reading a book when Tracy arrived.

Tracy was one of the women who visited Mrs Douglas regularly. She was a sexy medium-height mulatto in her late twenties. Her long, thick hair was dyed corn-yellow. She wore a lot of jewellery, drove a posh Volvo and used too much make-up on her pretty face.

Now she sat beside me on the sofa, hugged and kissed me. As usual she smelt of expensive French perfume.

"Listen to me carefully," she said, "I have been wanting to talk to you alone since the first day I met you. I am in love with you, not just because your cunt is the sweetest I have ever tasted. I just know we are meant for each other." Her eyes searched mine.

How could a woman, I thought, fall in love with another woman?

"I know," she added kindly, "all about Mr Douglas love of buggering women's asses. Do you like when he buggers your ass?" Her voice was compassionate and understanding.

I blushed – greatly ashamed – and said softly. "I hate it, but I can't leave unless I find a nice job." I trusted her.

"I can give you a job. But first I must tell you I am a whore." She said the word proudly.

I gaped at her with open incredulity.

"Don't be alarmed. I am not suggesting you become one. I want you to come live with me as my lover, friend and secretary-companion. I already have a live-in helper to cook, clean and wash."

"What work will I do?" I was suspicious.

"You will help me with my book-keeping, tidy the house, iron and shop for groceries. I need you. I am in love with you. Will you come?"

"Give me some time to think about it." I wasn't convinced her aim wasn't to recruit me for her business. Once I went to her home it might all become another nightmare. The thought of selling my body to different men each night seemed worse than being buggered by Mr Douglas.

"You will have a room that's as comfortable as the one you have here." She sounded sincere. "I am rich and I am not a street whore. I do my work at home. A few rich men by appointment only. I have two houses rented out.

"I inherited my three houses from my parents. They died when I was eighteen. It is hard to explain why I sell my body." She shrugged. "It seemed the most interesting job to me."

"Give me a week to think," I said,

"Okay." She was disappointed. "But believe me I do love you more than I thought I could love anyone." She wrote down her address and phone number and gave it to me saying, "If an emergency arises, phone or come see me."

Just then Mrs Douglas arrived.

I was tempted to go live with Tracy. She had sounded sincere. But I wasn't sure she had been. However, at the next Friday night orgy I was the victim of a most painful and humiliating scene.

Next morning I phoned Tracy and she came for me. I went to her home willing to be a whore. What the Douglases and their friends had done to me was far worse than prostitution.

Chapter 15

Tracy lived in a lovely two-storey house in Forrest Hills Gardens, about four miles from the Douglases, on the slopes of the Red Hills overlooking the city. The quarter-acre grounds surrounding her house were immaculately kept. From upstairs one had a breath-taking night view of the city. Upstairs consisted of two bathrooms and three bedrooms and a small unfurnished hall. Tracy occupied the master bedroom, which had its own bathroom. She gave me one of the other two bedrooms.

My room was as comfortable as the one I had had at the Douglases. The walls weren't papered, but there was a wall-to-wall carpet on the floor and a Chinese rug by the king size bed, which had a gorgeously carved headboard varnished in a rich brown, matching the rest of the furniture.

Downstairs consisted of a living room, dining room, den/library, kitchen, washroom, an apartment of two rooms, bathroom and tiny kitchen, occupied by Tracy's homosexual cousin and his lover, and the maid's apartment at the back.

Tracy's cousin, Harry, was a tall and muscular red-skinned twenty-five-year-old insurance salesman. His lover, Patrick, was a slim effeminate, eighteen-year-old mulatto young man who could've been described as a 'pretty man'. Patrick was a 'housewife', or rather, a 'houseman'.

The live-in helper was a fat, cheerful, black, middle-aged woman. In addition to looking after Tracy's housework and washing, she also washed for Patrick and Harry.

My last night with the Douglases had been a great terror, unforgettably horrid. I remember all of that day vividly. In the hour before noon, Mrs Douglas had lectured me on the ancient Greeks. Then, as it was a Friday, after lunch we went grocery shopping – as we did every Friday afternoon.

But at the orgy that night, there had been a difference, two

young men who I had never seen before. Both were black and in their mid-twenties.

As usual, the orgy began in the brightly illuminated living/dining room soon after the Taylors and Hustons arrived. Soft music flowed from the component set, marijuana, food – sandwiches and cakes – and drinks were plenty.

Wearing silver jewellery, my hairstyle elaborate, a lot of make-up and wearing black mesh stockings with suspenders, a red mini-skirt, a white tank top and red high-heeled shoes, I strode about with food and drink, lighting joints, and being groped and pinched by all hands.

By 9:00 p.m. everyone, except me,was high and those who weren't naked weren't far from it. (I never drank or smoked a lot at these orgies, since my main function was being a waitress.) The two young men were naked and I saw that they had huge manhoods, almost as large as Mr Douglas'.

Suddenly Mr Douglas stopped nibbling Mrs Huston's breasts and bellowed, "Now for our special attraction!"

What was it to be, I thought.

"Come, Carlene," Mr Douglas said, "you are the 'star' of our show."

I frowned. I had not been told about a special show. However, I was soon on my hands and knees, wearing only my stockings, suspenders and shoes, one of the young men's cock in my mouth, Mr Douglas in my cunt and the other young man in my ass. This wasn't the first time I was taking three cocks at once, so I wasn't alarmed. About half an hour passed before both young men climaxed, Mr Douglas didn't.

Before I could've regained my wits, I was handcuffed and bound on top of the coffee table. "What are you going to do?" I was terrified. Though we had played bondage games before, I now smelt danger in the air. "Please..."

"Don't be scared," Mrs Douglas soothed, "it's only a game. And you'll be getting a generous reward."

Before I could respond a dildo was forced into my mouth and

101

strapped around my head so I couldn't spit it out. Next a huge vibrator was shoved up my cunt and turned on. I was terrified. Then Mr Douglas used a whip to give my bottom ten lashes. Next he and the two young men buggered my ass without mercy. It was horrible, the dildo in my mouth made breathing difficult.

After this they took the dildo from my mouth and the vibrator from my cunt. They untied me from the coffee table, and forced me to lie on my back on an exercise mat. Then all the men fucked me. I just lay there crying, comforting myself with the thought that tomorrow I would go to Tracy, my body riddled with pain.

I was forced to my feet. The music was turned up and they began to chant, "Dance! Dance! Dance!..." They were stoned out of this world.

Dazed and tottering on my high heels, but seething with anger, I glared at their gleefully stoned faces.

"...Dance!" "Go! Dance! Baby dance for us." "Dance!"

A camera flashed twice. At me. I was swaying like a coconut tree in a strong breeze. Perhaps they thought I was dancing?

"She is tough!"

"Dance! Dance!"

"Perhaps tough girls don't dance!"

Their faces got very blurred. "I hate you all!" I hissed, before I fainted.

I awoke in my bed next morning feeling sore and aching all over. My first thought was, 'Tracy. Go phone her.' I got out of bed and, hit by a brief dizzy spell, I tottered before gaining my balance. Except for stockings and suspenders, I was naked. There was a large patch of blood on the bed, from my shredded asshole. My reflection in the mirror was horrible – my face a death mask, eyes swollen, hair a mess, my body bruised. My rear was criss-crossed with welts, and blood was caked between my legs and the cheeks of my rear. I stumbled to the bathroom and washed my face. This made me feel much better.

I put on my bathrobe and went to the living-dining room. It

was minutes before 8:00 a.m. The Douglases were still asleep. Tracy's helper answered my phone call, saying Tracy was sleeping.

"It's an emergency," I urged her. "Please go wake her. Tell her Carlene says it's an emergency."

A few minutes later Tracy was on the line sounding clearer than I had expected. "Carlene love, what's wrong?"

"Please come for me now," I sobbed. "Come now..."

"I am on my way, love. Are you hurt?"

"Not too bad."

"I am on my way, honey." She hung up.

I returned to my room, put on a dress and began to pack my clothing into two travelling bags. What the bags couldn't hold, I dumped on the bed.

Shortly afterwards I heard Tracy's Volvo stop at the gate. Then the dog was playing with her as she came up the driveway. I hurried to the front door and let her in – the very dog seemed amazed at how horrid I looked.

"What did they do to you?" Tracy cried angrily. She was wearing a house dress and slippers, and a tam covered her hair. I began to cry. She hugged me to her bosom.

The Douglases, naked and still half asleep, stumbled into the living room. They looked like something the cats had dragged in, but I was sure they weren't aching half as much as I was.

"What's going on?" he asked.

"Tracy?" she mumbled like an old crone.

"Carlene is coming with me," Tracy snarled. "What did you do to her, you pricks!"

It took several seconds for Tracy's words and ferocity to make sense to their soggy brains. Then they came fully wake. "Carlene whad...what does Tracy mean?" she asked.

"I am going to live with her!" I snapped indignantly.

"But why?" (He had the nerve to a ask!)

"To get away from your buggering her, you beast!" Tracy snapped.

"Tracy, how can you..."

"Come," Tracy said guiding me towards my room, "let's go get your things."

They followed us. "Carlene, you are ungrateful," she said. "And you, Tracy, are a fraud. You want her for your whoring business."

"Carlene knows I am a whore. She's coming as my lover and secretary. As usual, you'll soon find another young girl to help you satisfy your husband's love for female assholes!"

I carried one of my bags to Tracy's car, every step was sheer agony. Tracy made three trips with the rest of my belongings. We drove away.

When we arrived at Tracy's home, she gave me a warm bath. Then she cleaned and dressed my asshole. I slept all day. In the evening I told her what they had done to me. She was compassionate and maternal.

She was worried that my asshole had been badly damaged, and that perhaps I would develop an infection in my vagina. But, miraculously, I pulled through without having to see a doctor, thanks to the skill and care of Tracy, the helper, Tracy's cousin, Harry, and his lover.

Tracy treated me like a princess. But I knew I couldn't spend my life the way she wanted me to, as her life-long faithful lover. I needed a man to give me utter sexual satisfaction. Plus, I wanted to carve out a successful life by my own efforts; or at least try to succeed. But because she had helped me when I was in need of it, I decided to be her faithful lover for a fair amount of time. And I tried to be perfect at the few tasks she gave me.

She took no more than three clients each night, and only by appointment (she taught me how to arrange the appointments for her, and she never suggested I help entertain her clients). She didn't work on Thursday nights, and we always went to a restaurant then to a movie, play, or a lesbian club.

She showered me with gifts, though I told her not to – I knew I could leave her at any moment. She told me about her clients and their tastes – most of them told her their life stories and prob-

lems. The only sexual acts she didn't cater to was to allow herself to be bound or her body to be abused roughly – whipped, burned etc.

She had several clients who loved her to flog them – one middle-aged man who was impotent came to be whipped, to eat her cunt and nibble her breasts and toes. There were others who loved when she bound their limbs and made love to them. She allowed men to bugger her but, as she said, none of them were as large as Mr Douglas or had his incredible stamina to delay climax indefinitely.

"Mr Douglas," she snorted, "is a fuckin' robot. I have never met another like him."

She had three clients who came more than once each week, another three came at least once each week, and about a dozen who came by occasionally. They were all rich men and mostly middle-aged.

The appointments were spaced so as to give Tracy time to bathe and get dressed again between each. So the men rarely met each other.

Despite the 'official' method by which Tracy operated, I was glad she didn't try to include me.

But I got the feeling that one of her middle-aged clients was going to fall for me.

Chapter 16

Tracy Jenning was born and had grown up in Kingston. Her parents were a mulatto couple and she was their only child. The late Mr Jenning had been a very successful lawyer who had invested in real estate. Mrs Jenning had been a housewife and voluntary social worker.

Tracy admitted that she had been a spoilt child who received her every request and was never spanked. She had been a terror to servants and teachers, and a bit of a tomboy. Her parents had died together in a car crash when she was eighteen years old and about to enter university in the USA.

Tracy was so shattered by her parents untimely death she had put off going to university and went to live with her favourite aunt. Before long, she and her older cousin became lovers and she found that sex helped her depression. So she began to have sex with 'any and everybody', including girls. In 1971 when she turned twenty-one she inherited her parents' estate. She sold her parents' home and bought her Red Hills home, left her aunt's home, decided it was too late and unnecessary to go to university and began to sell her body to men to satisfy her seemingly insatiable sexual needs – why give it away when she could easily turn it into a very profitable career, she had reasoned. She had continued to engage in lesbianism, but never for money, because she loved its gentleness, and sex with women made her feel she was in control of her sex drive and could do without men. (I suspect that subconsciously she was angry at her father because he had been drunk on the night he and his wife died – he had been the driver.)

After I had been with Tracy for two months I knew I could trust her. I told her everything about my past and showed her my savings.

"My love," she cooed maternally, "you have had a rough past. And I am so happy you trust me enough to have told me all of it.

Stay with me for always and you will be safe. We are alike. Bisexuals. You can have as many men as you want. Just stay with me and don't get seriously involved with anybody else."

What she was asking of me would have been so easy to do, but I was obsessed with the desire to achieve financial success on my own. And this I wouldn't be able to do if I was to remain with Tracy.

True, she could afford to pay for me to gain a higher education, and I was sure she would do it if I asked, but she had done enough for me, and eventually I would tire of our lifestyle.

Yes, I mused, I must gain success by way of being the paramour of a wealthy middle-aged man, or a series of such men. But for as long as I lived with Tracy, I told myself, I would be her faithful lover and refrain from abusing her kindness.

Tracy and I went to Belfield on the day after my eighteenth birthday. The area had not changed much. But the lane on which I had lived was now paved, and there was electricity in my momma's house.

Momma was sitting on the verandah when the Volvo stopped at her gate. Tracy and I got out. Momma's eyes almost popped out of her head. Tracy and I were in jeans, T-shirts and sport shoes. I glanced around. It was all the same, momma's bamboo kitchen, out-house at the back, house the same.

"Hello, momma." My tone was pleasant and casual as if nothing had gone wrong with us. Momma was dumb with surprise. I introduced her to Tracy.

"Carlene," momma said, after exchanging greetings with Tracy who she now turned to and added unsteadily, "Miss Jenning, I give her up as dead."

I was moved. Clearly, momma had really missed me. "Momma," I soothed, "I am sorry. But I thought it best not to write or visit until now."

She sighed, a long-suffering sigh of relief. Then she went inside for an extra chair – there were two verandah chairs already available.

When we were all seated she said, "So what yu doing since yu leave?"

"First I worked as a helper. But now I am working in Tracy's store and I live at her house. She has no family and was alone in a big house since she and her husband were divorced three years ago." Tracy had instructed me to tell these lies.

"Carlene is intelligent," Tracy said, "and very honest. And it is so hard to find honest workers and friends these days. She is just the type of person I would've wanted as a sister. So I told her to come live at my house as a friend."

"I am glad to hear that she is honest," momma said. I got the feeling she didn't believe I was working in a store. Most likely she thought Tracy and I were top flight whores. But throughout the hours I was to stay that day, momma didn't try to take me aside to quiz me and she didn't mention Kevin. And it was clear that, though she suspected Tracy was a whore, momma sensed that Tracy sincerely cared about me and was capable of protecting me. (I am sure momma didn't suspect Tracy and I were lovers.)

At 1:15 p.m. my stepdaddy and my brothers came home from the bush. My twelve-year-old brother looked fourteen, and had a bold air about him. The younger, now eight, was shy.

Tracy and the Volvo made daddy jittery. Like momma he looked no older than when I had run away. After greeting Tracy he said in a thin voice, "Carlene yu worry me an' yu momma real bad. But we know it was our fault why yu left."

"Every day a blame meself," momma intoned.

"Anyhow," daddy added, "a glad to see yu okay an' doing well."

"No need to worry anymore." I smiled at him but my eyes flashed him a brief message of my dislike and desire for vengeance. I would've loved to choke the bastard. He and the Douglases, I thought fervently, and Carl Bell would someday pay for their cruelty to me.

I asked momma for my birth certificate, and got it. Now I was truly an adult, I thought wryly.

Before we left Belfield at 5:00 p.m. I visited my aunts. I gave momma $350 and each brother $20 before I left.

That night I had the recurring dream about Carl and myself at sea (it recurred at least once every two months). I dismissed it, as usual, as being stupid and senseless. After all, I mused, I surely wouldn't be attempting my revenge at sea.

I didn't tell Tracy about this unexplainable dream.

A few weeks later Tracy began to give me driving lessons in the afternoons. After my first week of lessons she said, "You were born to drive, just as you were born to give ultimate satisfaction in bed." She was looking at me with eyes which were clouded with desire. "Yours is the only pussy that tastes like honey."

I rolled my eyes and chided histrionically, "You are always saying that silly thing."

"It's true."

"Yours is just as sweet."

"No, love. Yours is the only pussy that drips honey. I have tasted my own many times."

I giggled. "How did you taste your own pussy? With your finger?"

"I was good at gymnastics up to my parents' death, thin as a straw and very supple. And was into yoga via reading. At fourteen I found that I could eat my virgin cunt."

I gaped. Incredulous.

Sounded wild. Was it possible?

On the last Monday afternoon in May, Tracy and I went to a bank on Constant Spring Road. It was my intention to open an account with all of my savings, which now stood at $8,500. I had expected it to be a pleasant experience.

But it turned out to be a nightmare. A real terror.

Chapter 17

It was a cold, drab-looking bank with potted plants along the wall of glass at the front. I was lying on my stomach beside Tracy on the cold floor. I was terrified, my heart beat loud in my ears. Would Tracy and I be shot? Killed? Was this happening because I had once helped in an armed robbery? Why the hell don't you pray?...

Tracy and I had entered the bank at 2:15 p.m. I had joined the short line at the window labelled 'New Accounts'. My money was in my large handbag. The bank wasn't crowded.

I had been in the bank for less than five minutes when I heard a restrained, brief scream (the type where the screamer used a hand or bag to cut off what had hardly been a scream from the start). I turned and saw several men waving pistols, large ugly ones. I thought it was the Trigger Squad. But next moment I knew it wasn't my old pals.

The gunmen ordered everyone to lie, face down, with eyes closed.

'Dear God,' I now prayed, 'don't let them harm anybody, especially Tracy...' My thoughts flashed back to the day the Squad and I had robbed the store downtown.

'But God, you know I was forced to take part, which was why I had run away from the Squad as soon as I could.'

I peeped at Tracy. She looked calm. I didn't try to look at the gunmen, and I closed my eyes once again. My heart skipped a beat and I held my breath when I felt my handbag being yanked away. I was wise enough not to resist.

There, gone, was my $8,500. Still, almost half of it had been stolen from someone else, I thought. Thief from thief, God laugh?

I lay there rigid for another minute, that seemed like hours, when a rush of voices began. The robbers were gone. It had seemed as if the gunmen had spent hours, but in fact the robbery had taken no more than five or six minutes.

I got up shakily. Tracy hugged me maternally. "Don't be sad," she coaxed, "you'll soon be able to open an account."

All around us there were indignant hysterical voices. The disarmed policeman was shouting that everyone should remain until an investigation squad arrived. But Tracy and I left with half of the customers.

From the discussions around us I learned that there had been five gunmen, all dressed in expensive suits. They had entered the bank separately, posing as customers. As soon as the last entered through the door, all five had pulled our their automatic pistols, the one by the entrance quickly disarming the policeman on guard by the door.

The robbers had robbed the tellers and several customers, including me. Nobody had been hurt, no shots fired.

On the way home I considered the irony that God had ordained the robbers to take away my money because almost half of it was stolen money. Had the bank robbery been a divine act?

But others, I reasoned, had been robbed so it seemed to have been a stroke of bad luck. Surely God wouldn't have punished so many others because of me? And, after all, God was very understanding. He knew I had been forced to take part in the robbery with the Squad and that I couldn't have returned the money to the store owners without risking a prison term and being earnestly hunted by the Squad.

Could it have been, I wondered, that God was saying I should have left my share of the loot with the Squad?

I never did decide conclusively if that bank robbery had been a divine act against me.

As Tracy had said, a few months later I did open a bank account. At the same bank where I had been robbed. (Daring fate?) My first deposit was $1,600. Then, because Tracy was giving me $100 each week and I had no expenses, I was thereafter able to add at least $300 to my account each month.

I had been with Tracy for six months when one of her clients

began to show interest in me. He complimented me on my beauty, charm, intelligence and clothings. Sometimes he'd pinch my bosom or give me a light slap on my rear or hold me and grope my cunt – only when Tracy wasn't present – and I would protest half-heartedly, pouting and narrowing my eyes provocatively.

Then he began to quiz Tracy about my role in her house.

"Mr Chin is always asking about you lately," Tracy told me calmly, "as if he has just begun to notice how lovely you are." (He was one of her weekly customers.) "I told him we are lovers. He doesn't disapprove of two women making love, but he isn't the type of man who gets pleasure from such acts."

I was silent, acting bored. But I was excited. We were on the balcony that ran along the back of the upstairs and from where one had a thrilling night view of the city below. Now it was afternoon.

"So what, do you like him?" Tracy asked, her eyes searching. "I won't mind if you have an affair with him, so long as it's not for money and you remain here."

"I am not interested in men now."

But I had not fooled her. "I want you to be happy." Her voice was sincere. She knew I wouldn't be content with only lesbianism for long. Calmly she told me all she knew about him, which was a lot; he had been her weekly customer for the past four years.

What she told me made my heart race excitedly. Mr Chin was the type of man I was after. He was rich, middle-aged, generous and dominated his wife. And, as a bonus, he wasn't a 'weirdo' in bed and had no fetish.

A perfect catch.

Thereafter, whenever he was due for an appointment with Tracy, I took extra care about my appearance. From reading, I had learnt that, usually, successful middle-aged men preferred their young mistress to be moderately intelligent and to act as if she was gaining knowledge from all he said. With Mr Chin I acted thus.

Chapter 18

Mr David Chin was a forty-seven-year-old half-black, half-Chinese. He was married to a mulatto lady and was devoted to their three teenaged children. He owned and operated a thriving real estate business, and had shares in several companies, was a leading race horse owner and the head of a marijuana smuggling ring.

He was a short, dapper man with a slight paunch which went well with his big-boned, heavy-set body. A handsome man whose curly jet-black hair and low, neat beard gave him a distinguished look.

His Chinese father, a small shop keeper in rural Westmoreland, had been an outcast of the Chin clan because he had married a black woman – David's mother (in those days Jamaican Chinese had been very clannish). David was the only child of this, then unusual, union. David was twenty when his father died, and he came to Kingston leaving the shop with his mother.

By the time he got married at thirty, David was well on his way to riches. Now he was a wealthy man with powerful political connections.

Mr Chin was booked to see Tracy from 6:30 p.m. to midnight on New Year's Day, 1979. By now I knew he was yearning to make love to me, but was convinced I was a hopeless lesbian. But I had decided to let him know I wanted him. Before January was over, I was sure, I would bed him and use his pent-up lust for me to help chain his balls and heart to my cunt.

Tracy and I were sitting on the verandah when he arrived at 6:20 p.m. He parked beside Tracy's car in the dual carport – Harry and Patrick had left in their car a few minutes before. It was now dusk.

"Good evening girls. You are both a pleasing feast for the eyes on this first day of '79."

"Good evening, Mr Chin." I gave him my sexiest smile.

"I have a headache," Tracy sighed,

"Let's go in out of the chilly air," he suggested paternally. We went inside and locked the front door. He and Tracy sat down on the elegant red sofa. I sat down in a nearby armchair.

We were in the airy and richly furnished living room which was dominated by shades of red and brown. The large chandelier bathed us with light.

"Is the pain bad?" he asked Tracy. "I was looking forward to a wild night. But if you are ill, well," (he shrugged disappointedly) "you know I am not cruel.

"It's not so bad," she said.

"Why not," he said with an amused grin at me, "allow me to bed your lovely companion." It was a jesting statement.

My heart did an excited flip, and I couldn't keep an anxious smile and excited flush from my face. Tracy glanced at me and saw my excitement. (Who could've failed to see?) She smiled. I looked away and met David's eyes which held a look of amazed incredulity – clearly he had thought I was afraid of, or disliked, sex with men, and now here I was, showing clearly that I desired him.

"Of course, you can have her," Tracy said earnestly, mulatto face flushed excitedly, "if she wants to. But I can tell you she won't do it for money."

"Well, Carlene, what do you say?"

His voice I would've described as being ecstatically anxious. "If you don't help us out I shall have to go away very gloomy or give Tracy a miserable time."

I was looking at Tracy. "Go ahead," she said, "you want to."

"I'll do it, but I am sure I won't be as good as Tracy." I had intended to sound calm, but I realized I sounded as eager as a nymphomaniac just out from prison.

"As Tracy can tell you," he beamed, "I don't go to bed only to get pleasure. I love to give at least as much as I get. Which is why," he grinned, "I wouldn't want to go to bed with two women since I wouldn't be able to give as much as I would be sure to get."

I glowed. He was better than I could've hoped for, perfect.

David and I went up the carpeted stairway. At the top I turned and looked down at Tracy. She waved and blew me a kiss.

In romantic silence David and I rushed to my bedroom and tore off our clothes. I turned on my bedside lamp, low, just enough light to make him see me clearly. We jumped onto the bed. I gave him my best.

He was great. A gentle lover who could withhold himself. I had three orgasms before he climaxed. Then we lay quietly and close for a while.

"Did you really have three orgasms or are you good at faking?" His voice was lovingly gentle. "Just as you were able, for months, to make me think you didn't like men sexually and had no sexual experience with us."

"I haven't had a man for a year. And I didn't want to interrupt Tracy's business." I was pouting sexily. Then shyly, "I have been dreaming about you. And you are the best I have ever had."

"I am greatly honoured," he said graciously, like an ancient Chinese character. "It has been a long time since I enjoyed sex so much. I had to use my reserve will-power to hold back my climax for so long, which I usually do without much effort."

I beamed, elated. Transfigured into a sensual goddess.

"Tracy," he added, "told me she took you away from a couple who were overworking you."

God bless Tracy, I thought, for sparing my dignity. I nestled closer to David. "That's why I have been faithful to her."

"Do you intend to stay with her?"

"Until I find a nice man, like you, who loves me."

"You have found him," he said passionately, and kissed me, his hand moving all over my quivering, naked body.

"Your intelligence and manners" he said, "makes it hard to believe you didn't go to a posh girls' school."

Triumphant ecstasy maddened me. I attacked his naked body which suddenly looked golden in the soft light from the cream-colour shaded lamp on my beside table. The cool breeze which

was blowing through the open windows and door, that led to the balcony, heightened my passion.

My second performance out-shone the first.

Afterwards we lay contentedly spent for almost a minute, my head on his firm, hairy chest. How grand it would have been, I mused, to be his mistress for even a year.

"You are a wild one," he suddenly said kindly. "Aren't you a bit chilly?"

"Yes, a bit." We got under the sheet.

"I never thought," he said, "I could ever find a girl your age to rival Tracy's skill in bed. You are how old, eighteen?"

"Yes, sir. Nineteen in May this year."

"You a May girl. Taurus?"

"Yes, Mr Chin."

He chuckled. "Here we are in bed and you calling me 'sir' and 'Mr Chin'."

"I respect you a lot and wouldn't call you by your first name unless you told me to. It's not your age or money. It's what you are, almost like a god." That should impress him – reading had taught me that all middle-aged men had the ego of ten-year-old boys.

"You are a special girl," he beamed in the semi-dark. "From now on call me David."

"Okay."

"Would you like to be my woman?"

I glowed brilliantly. Ecstasy threatened to sizzle me. My aim had been achieved, almost effortlessly. I heard the voices of a thousand dead paramours singing praises to my name. "Oh, David! Yes!" My voice was unsteady with emotion.

"I am going to give you a furnished apartment. The only laws I will lay down for you to obey are that you musn't get pregnant or see other men. And never try to disrupt my family life. Be faithful and obedient and I will give you the best, money to spend and show you ways to make a fortune for yourself. But if you ever betray my trust or try to disrupt my family life, you will find that I can be very rough. When can you leave here?"

"Anytime, my love!"

"Let's make it next Saturday. And, yes, I won't mind you seeing Tracy."

I went for his body again, and soon had him fully aroused. It was as if I was making love to a fleshy vault of money – clear pictures of wads of money flashed across the screen of my mind. And when at last he spilled his seed deep inside me, I thought of liquid gold.

It was 10:30 p.m. when we left my bedroom. We found Tracy in the living room dozing on the sofa. She woke up shading her eyes from the bright overhead light.

"Are you better, Tracy?" Mr Chin asked her.

"Much"

"Well, I am going now. Bye, Carlene love."

"Bye, David."

Tracy cocked an eyebrow. He left. She asked no questions, and said she would be able to see the man who would be coming at 12:30 a.m. We sat in the living room talking of this and that, nothing about David and me.

I had decided not to tell her my joyous news until next day. I knew she would be greatly disappointed, perhaps very angry. But I couldn't withhold telling her until the last moment. She had been so loving and kind to me, I had to take the risk that she would order me out of her house tomorrow.

Chapter 19

Tracy awoke at 10:00 a.m. next morning. I had been up from 6:00 a.m. planning how I should break my news to her. I had put off breakfast until she was ready to eat.

After breakfast we went to sit on the back verandah, looking down on the shimmering city below. It was a very hot day, the air still. In the distance the sea was a sparkling blue.

"Tracy," I said after taking a deep breath, "I have enjoyed our year together and I will always have a special love for you, and be your lover for as long as you want." I paused. Her face was twisted with anxiety. It took a lot of effort for me to continue looking into her eyes as I added: "David wants me to be his mistress so I will be leaving soon. He is giving me a furnished apartment."

Her face was drained, and for several seconds she was dumbfounded. "Why can't you stay here!" she cried desperately. "You would have me when business makes it impossible for him to see you!"

"Tracy, David and I couldn't have an affair in your home." My voice was small and thick. It was painful to see how much I was hurting her. But even if she had offered me a million dollars I just wouldn't have been able to live how she wanted me to.

"Darling, do you think I mind losing David as a customer?" Her lips trembled. "I am glad he loves you so much he wants you as his mistress. He is kind and will be true to you, I want you to be happy."

"I just have to launch out on my own for a while." I was begging her to understand. "Do something for myself, by my own efforts."

"But darling, sometimes he won't be able to visit you for days. You'll be alone, lonely. It's not as if you are foolishly in love with him."

"I'll come stay with you when he is away or busy for days. Plus I will visit you regularly otherwise. That's if you want me. David said he won't mind if you and I continue being lovers."

"It won't be the same as having you here." Her tone was wistful, eyes filmed by tears. She leaned across to hold my hand. (We were in close but separate cushioned patio chairs.) Eyes bright with desperate hope, she suggested: "I'll get rid of Harry and Patrick, and give you their apartment. That'll give you the privacy you need."

What was there so different about my cunt that made men and women willing to go to great lengths to control me for their lusts?

"Please," I said firmly, "don't let this be more difficult than it already is. It wouldn't be fair to Harry and you need a man to live on your premises."

She sighed despondently, dabbed at her eyes with a handkerchief, smiled weakly and said, "Okay. I guess it's not so bad since we can meet often. And in case of trouble you can come back to me. Your room will be waiting."

Just then Harry and Patrick came out of their apartment into the backyard. "Hi, girls," Patrick sang.

That night I had my recurring nightmare about Carl and me at sea. It seemed, I mused, I would continue having that stupid dream until I was able to hurt that bastard. Someday I would find a way to satisfy my lust for revenge against him...and daddy, and the Douglases.

Mr Chin came for me at 8:00 a.m. the following Saturday. He had not returned since New Year's night, but had phoned me many times. Now I packed my suitcase and two travelling bags of clothes and my nine pairs of shoes and slippers in the trunk of his Benz. I placed my hats and handbags on the back seat.

Oh, I was on cloud nine. High on triumph and hopes of success.

Half asleep, Tracy was pleasant to David and kissed me goodbye. Clutching my jewellery case I got into the Benz.

David drove away. I felt like a princess.

My scheming, after over three years of preparation, had begun to pay.

The furnished apartment was on the top floor of a new six-storey building David owned in the New Kingston area. None of the other tenants, groundsman and night watchman knew he was the owner. I was the first person to live in the apartment he gave me; most of the other apartments were already occupied.

The car park was between the building and the street. The ground floor consisted of the lobby, launderette and a two-bedroom apartment. The first floor held two three-bedroom apartments. The second, third and fourth floors each housed three two-bedroom units. The top floor housed one two-bedroom and two one-bedroom units – I had one of the one-bedroom units.

At nights there was a watchman in the lobby who was linked to each apartment and the nearest police station. In the days there was a groundsman who kept the grounds swept, the pool clean and was also a sort of a watchman.

My apartment, like all the others, was air-conditioned, carpeted, the walls papered and comfortably furnished with dark-stained cedar and velvet-cushioned furniture.

My living room walls were papered blue; the dining room walls white with red and blue floral patterns; the bedroom's wall paper was a pale pink; a thick reddish-brown wall-to-wall carpet throughout; bathroom all pink; and the kitchen all yellow. The living room had French windows that led to a balcony which faced the road. French windows led from the dining room to a balcony which overlooked a pool and tennis court in the backyard where there was also a very green and neat lawn bordered with flowers.

Boy, was I thrilled with my new home.

As soon as we arrived at my posh nest, David and I made passionate love on the sheet-less bed. Afterwards we went to a nearby shopping centre where we bought sheets, two pillows and cases, towels, pots, crockery and silverware.

When we returned to my new home I asked, "David, should we be so bold in public together?"

He smiled. "My wife is eight years older than me and knows

I would never forsake her or our children. She doesn't care about my life outside the home. And she was never a highly sexed person. Now she's almost like a mother to me."

We had another 'quickie' on the unmade bed, took a quick shower, got dressed and left for the track: I hadn't unpacked. We stopped at a nearby restaurant for lunch.

It was 2:00 p.m. when we arrived at the track and the second race was about to start. David had only two horses on the programme that day – Swift-legs in the 3rd, Royal Boy in the 5th. A feeling of belonging gripped me as we got out of the Benz in the officials' car park, where all places were reserved, as if I had been born and bred at the track, though I knew almost nothing about horse racing.

"David darling, first thing I want to do is put a small bet on your horses."

He called a young man and sent him to place my bets – $20 on each horse.

"Today isn't an important day for me," David said, "so we'll go watch a few races, then I'll take you across to the stables to meet my trainer and horses." He steered me to the VIP box where he had three permanently reserved seats. I was determined to make him proud of me when I met his friends. But I wasn't nervous, I was, in fact, thrilled. Tracy had assured me, and I knew she had been sincere, that my speech and manners were now better than most members of the Jamaican upper class.

I swirled into the VIP box as if I were a princess. All the men, most of whom were middle-aged stared at me with open lust; half the women were young, obviously daughters and mistresses. I was wearing skin-tight blue pants, a red tube-top and white low-heeled slippers. My make-up was moderate, nails lacquered red and my hair in the blue silk scarf, and I was all decked out in silver. (A pity that most women don't know that silver is sexier than gold.)

It was obvious that David was well respected amongst these kings of the track – owner, trainers, stewards and major share-

holders of, and officials in, the group which owned the premises: I was introduced to many that day.

"David, my boy," remarked a fat middle-aged Chinaman, "must you always out-do us? Now we'll have to go hunt a girl as lovely as yours." His Chinese wife pinched him, her face dark. He ignored her.

"Born with the luck of a bishop," sighed a grey-haired mulatto, winking at me. "Honey, if David ever ill-treats you, come see me." Like the other women, his model-looking girlfriend glared at me.

I cocked my head provocatively like Ava Gardner and beamed a prehistorically sexy smile like Racquel Welch in 'One Million Years B.C.' I allowed a dramatic moment to pass, clearly showing I intended to speak, before I said in a sexily throaty voice like Marilyn Monroe's, "Perhaps I won't wait for him to ill-treat me."

"Are you," David said to me in mock anger, "Trying to get me to kill my friends."

"Wouldn't blame you, my boy," said another fat Chinaman. "Friends can't take you up to bite clouds."

Laughter from the men; the women grew darker.

In addition to impressing David's friends and stirring the juices of all his male pals – he had female friends – I also won $25 on Royal Boy who had placed third; Swift-legs ran out.

Being David's mistress was a grand life. He showered me with expensive gifts and gave me enough money so I could add to my bank account regularly. We went to the best restaurants and night clubs. Sometimes when he was going on overnight business trips to the North Coast he took me along. And, of course, we went to the race track on most Wednesdays and Saturdays – at times he took his family, leaving me behind. Whenever he went abroad he always brought me exotic works of art.

I did my best to please him, in and out of bed. He loved my cooking and jokes, so I always had a meal ready and jokes on the tip of my tongue. He spent at least two full nights with me each week. I was able to visit Tracy regularly and slept at her house whenever I was sure David wouldn't be coming that night.

122

Tracy and I were still lovers, and true to her word, she didn't take in another girl to replace me – she didn't, had never, needed a secretary. She paid me regular afternoon visits and we did most of our shopping together. By the end of 1979 I was winning a fair amount of money at the races, and was the belle of the VIP box (David didn't mind my harmless flirting). My bank account now stood at $20,000.

I was on my way to riches.

One night while we were eating one of my best cooked meals by candle light on my front balcony, I said, "David, honey, I am winning so much money at the track, thanks to you, and have no rent to pay, I think I should cut down on the amount of money you give me each week."

Would my subtle act pay off?

He gazed at me incredulously for suspended seconds, his eyes soft in the candle light. Then he reached across the small circular table to hold my hand and said softly, "You really are a special girl. I have never known another girl who would have said that. I assure you I have more than enough money to spend freely and still leave a fortune for each of my children. And I do love you. So don't feel guilty about taking what money I give you."

Triumph! My finesse had worked.

"That's a load off my mind. Lately I have been thinking I should get a job."

"No need, my love," he responded quickly. "A job would cut down on our time together. What you must do is read books about accounting and business management for the day when you'll have enough money to open a business."

At that moment I came close to falling in love with him.

I took his advice and began to read books on accounting and business management. And his generosity increased. I was really on my way to success.

Suddenly my thoughts began to reach out to the Trigger Squad. This was a premonition.

But first I was to meet Carl Bell again.

Chapter 20

I was still having the recurring dream about Carl and me. At least one night every two months. But I didn't think about how I would react if we met when I was alone. I only knew my revenge against him was years away.

Shortly before noon on a sunny Monday in mid-March, 1980 I took a taxi to the nearest shopping centre. I was in need of a few cosmetics. As I got out of the taxi I saw Carl Bell standing on the covered walkway gazing at me. He was wearing navy-blue pants and a white bush jacket with a name tag on the left breast, and he had a small, black leather bag.

The taxi drove away. For several dark seconds Carl and I stared at each other. Rooted. Time stopped. First his eyes were speculative, then they shone with delight as a wide grin split his face in two.

At first, I felt no specific emotion. But when he grinned my heart expanded and a warm ecstatic feeling, which I couldn't subdue, flooded me.

"Hello, Carlene." His voice was warm and cozy, causing my pulse to race excitedly.

How come I was acting as if I was overjoyed to see the scheming bastard? I hated him. What the hell was wrong with me?

Still, I couldn't keep a smile from my face and the gladness from my voice when I said, "Hi, Carl."

God have mercy on my confused soul. I was like two persons in one as I stepped up on to the walkway.

"Carlene you are looking wonderful. I have been so worried that I would never see you again." He was talking fast, face excited. "I knew you had left the Douglases but couldn't find out where you went."

"Why should you want to see me?" Why was my voice unsteady and my body trembling? Why couldn't I glare at him, use a cold voice, make him know I despised him?

He sighed. His eyes turned wistful. "You never did believe I love you." His voice was shaky. "For that I blamed myself. I wronged you. I shouldn't have forced you to be my lover. Please forgive me." Was he being sincere? Of course not, another voice whispered, don't you know the words 'forgive me' are always at the tip of men's tongues, from the day they are born? The bastard!

"No need to pretend." I had wanted to sound icy, but I only managed to sound calm. "No trick is going to get you between my legs again " (I still wasn't icy) "so stop acting."

A wounded look came on his face. Did I see signs of tears? I looked away, my mind in turmoil, totally bewildered – glad, yet sad, that I had wounded him.

He held up his hands, bag and all, in surrender. "All my fault," he mumbled. "All my fault."

Why did I feel ashamed. Yes, pain rent my soul. "Let's forget about the past." I was overwhelmed by an urge to change the subject. (Why didn't I just walk away?) "Tell me what you are doing now. You are in medical school it seems?" I suddenly remembered that we were on a public walkway, so I glanced around. The plaza was almost empty.

"Yes, I am in med-school now," he was saying, voice calm. "I am having a hard time finding a book I need. I came to the bookstore here. But they don't have it."

"I am glad you are in med-school." Dear God, corny one liners like a nervous virgin schoolgirl.

"What are you doing with yourself? First let's go have lunch," he took my bare arm, "then you can tell me what you have been up to." He was already guiding me towards the only restaurant in this one-storeyed, three-sided plaza.

I knew I should decline and wanted to say so, but the words were stuck in my throat, so I minced along on my high-heeled slippers, his hands on my naked arm sending a fire through my body. What was wrong with me? This wasn't how it should be. Perhaps I was dreaming?

The restaurant was small and cozy, the blue and white linen-

covered table a bit too close. But the orange-coloured cushioned chairs were comfortable and the food and service fairly good. Low jazz music flowed from hidden speakers. We arrived with the first surge of lunchers from nearby offices – middle-class workers in their neat suits, loud ties and smart skirt suits.

Carl and I ate in silence amid the jazz which was now background for a buzz of office gossip, romantic confessions, boasts, sports talk, complaints about spouses and the boss.

I nibbled at my steak and vegetables. (He was doing fine.) My behaviour and thoughts had me puzzled and scared. Here I was lunching with a man I was supposed to, or should, or did, hate. A man I had been planning to hurt in revenge someday. And what about the recurring dream? Even it said that I hated this young man.

Forget about the damn silly dream, a voice in my head screamed.

Could, I mused, hatred make one feel light-hearted and sexy?... You don't really hate him, I reasoned, you only dislike him for having exploited you sexually, and you want to punish him for having done so. Why not? Even mothers punish children for wrongs. The law also punishes law breakers.

But, I thought, could dislike make a girls' clit twitch each time the man she disliked smiled at her? Would sitting down to lunch with him make her cunt damp and her nipples hard?

Good thing I was wearing a bra, I thought, under my thin body blouse. Was my body betraying me because he had fucked me many times when I was at his house? A sort of a sexual tie that had nothing to do with the mind?

At the end of our meal he said, "Now tell me about you."

"Not much to tell." My voice was husky. I went into an unnecessary round of throat clearing and was able to subdue my physical emotions. "After I left the Douglases, I found another job for a year. Now I have a man who loves and supports me."

"I am not surprised. You were born with a special aroma. Only a fool wouldn't love you."

"My man is middle-aged and married." Was I, unconsciously, trying to make him jealous? Or was it all a bad dream? Or a lousy script?

"I am glad," he beamed, "your man isn't single and young. Do you live together?"

"No."

"Ah! So there is hope for me yet!"

"Hope for what?"

He leaned towards me. "Hope that someday you'll marry me."

I sighed. Exasperated, yet proud. Of course, I knew he was only trying to 'rope-in' my cunt once more. "Don't bother with silly tricks." My voice was casual.

"Okay," He held up his hands. "I won't say that again, though I am earnest."

I avoided his searching eyes. "I have to go now. I am in a hurry. And please allow me to pay."

"No way."

"If you truly love me, let me pay." My God, what had made me say that?

He beamed. "In that case, I will swallow my pride."

"I mean," I blurted shakily, "you are a student. My man is very rich and gives me a lot of money."

"I can see that," he said, eyeing my gold chain with its ruby pendant.

I signalled for the bill, paid and we left. Perhaps now I would awake from this horribly muddled dream.

"Your walk," he said, "is what one would expect of the ancient goddesses."

We were outside on the pavement. "You don't walk like an ordinary doctor." Dear me, who had written this script?

He said, "I'll drive you home. I have mom's car."

"No, I'll take a taxi. Plus I have some shopping to do."

"I can wait. And I promise you I won't visit you if you say I mustn't." He sounded earnest. "One thing I do ask is that if you are ever in need of a friend, please call on me."

Warmth flooded me. I nodded, bewildered by my emotions. We went to a department store and I bought the few items I needed. Then he drove me home, talking about med-school on the way.

When he stopped in front of my building he said, "Remember your promise to call if you need a friend to talk to."

"Yes," I squeaked softly. "I will." I got out. He drove away, without a backward glance. Why did I feel empty and sad and small? Why were tears threatening to flow?

Confused and angry at myself, I turned and ran into the building – luckily there was nobody about. On the seemingly endless ride up in the elevator, I began to cry, hating myself for doing so, but unable to stop the tears from flowing, my thoughts an utter muddle.

As soon as I entered my apartment I went to lie down on my bed staring unseeingly up at the ceiling trying to straighten out my mind. What were my true feelings, I mused, for Carl? I could not find the answer, but had to admit that my body wanted him.

Then I realized that unconsciously I was rubbing my crotch. Ecstasy overwhelmed me. I unbuttoned my skirt, loosened my body blouse and put my hand inside my panties. And – believe this – sobbing, I masturbated (the first time in years) despising but wanting Carl, sobbing his name, whimpering in ecstasy, finally choking on his name and my tears amidst those of a drawn-out orgasm.

For days I pondered on my confusing emotions towards Carl (when I was with David or Tracy I forgot about him and was light-hearted). But my emotions remained a muddled puzzle. Thinking about him didn't cause me to masturbate again. I knew that if he came to see me I couldn't keep him from my bed. Fortunately, I wasn't to see him for many months and forgot him after a week. But not because I had come to a conclusion concerning him.

It was my violent reunion with the Trigger Squad that forced Carl Bell from my mind for a long time.

Chapter 21

The Monday following my dreamlike encounter with Carl I took a taxi to one of the shopping centres on Constant Spring Road. I was headed for a ladies' shop which was having a sale. When I got out of the taxi, the car park was half full, and the mid-morning skies overcast. I was dressed casually in jeans, low-heeled pumps and a cotton blouse.

I looked up to the first floor of the two-storeyed centre where the store I was heading for was located. It seemed full. First day of sale. I walked across the three-sided carpark/plaza towards one of the stairways. I was a bit nervous, I didn't like coming to this area because I knew this was where the Squad shopped and I didn't want to meet them. But its being a Monday I knew it was very unlikely that I would run into any of them. Still, I was on the look-out because lately they had been in my thoughts and dreams. I was half-way up the narrow stairs, ahead of several housewives, when half of the Squad appeared at the head of the stairs – Shut, Head, Ray, Susan and Evan.

I froze. But the boys didn't. As soon as they realized it was me, they were leaping down towards me.

Run! my mind screamed. But I was rooted by dread. Then they were on me. The women behind me screamed and fled back down the stairs.

"So we meet again!" Shut sneered, squeezing one of my breasts forcefully.

I groaned in pain and tried to step back. But Head held my arm and hair.

"We going teach yu a lesson," Head said bitterly.

"The Squad don't like deserters." This from Ray. The girls were silent still at the top of the stairs.

I struggled, in vain. Shut's fist slammed into my cherry coloured mouth, splitting a lip. I saw Ray take out his knife and knew he was going to mar my face. Head punched the wind out of me and I sagged.

Then next moment I heard a blessed voice, "Police!" from below, followed by a shot.

My assailants flew up the stairs. I crumpled against the wall gasping. The policeman didn't give chase. He came to my side and gave me a supporting arm. I leaned against his laundry-smelling uniform. A crowd had gathered and were murmuring.

"You'll soon be okay, miss," the cop repeated soothingly.

"Thank you," I was able to say at last. "Thank you, officer."

"Let's go sit in the lounge upstairs," he suggested, "until you regain your wits." He cleared a path through the crowd, and led me to the lounge. I gulped the water I was given.

"Those were some terrible boys." The dimly lit and comfortably furnished lounge was half empty. "They split your lip."

I dabbed at my throbbing and swelling lips with a handkerchief. It wasn't a bad split.

"Jus' las' week," he said with a western accent, "my colleagues lock up two of them for murder, but had to let them go." He was a short, thick, black man about twenty-two years old. "Did they steal anything from you?"

"No." I was still trembling. "They were angry because I ignored their advances." I didn't want him to suspect I knew them.

"Listen, miss. Yu look like a nice girl. My advice to yu is to forget the incident. If yu agree I won't report the incident. But if yu want me to report it so that yu can press charges, yu may run into more problems with those boys. I know them. They are dangerous. Very. It's best if yu forget the matter, and don't come to this area without a man to protect yu."

I nodded. "I'll do as you say."

"That's best."

"Would you like a drink?"

"No thanks. Too early. What you going to do now?"

"Go home." We left the lounge. He helped me find a taxi. Before I got in I took $50 from my bag. "Please take this and buy a drink."

"No, miss. What I did was my duty." His voice was calm and proud.

"Please take it and buy a drink. It will make me feel good."

"Miss, a policeman..."

"Please," I pleaded. "I won't get in the taxi if you don't accept my gift."

"Come on," the taxi driver said.

Reluctantly, the policeman took the note. I got into the taxi.

I told neither Tracy nor David about my close shave with the Squad. I told them I had fallen in the bath. I wouldn't be going back to any of the Constant Spring Road shopping centres, unless it was with David who always had his licensed gun and was a karate expert.

And, of course, I now added the male members of the Squad to my hit list. At the very top of it.

Chapter 22

Life returned to normal. In June I got my driver's licence, and David began to allow me to sometimes drive his Benz when we were going out. I began to drive Tracy's Volvo all over town.

David took his family to Canada for the last two weeks of the year, for a 'white Christmas'. I spent my Christmas with Tracy. Then on the 27th we went to Belfield. I drove the last half of the journey.

Momma, daddy, my two brothers, one of my aunts and several of my cousins were on the verandah when I stopped the Volvo at the gate. They gaped, eyes popping. Me driving, and a Volvo at that!

Tracy left in the afternoon and was to return for me on the 30th. For three days I was going to torment daddy with my curvy body, this was the main reason for my stay – because I didn't want to hurt momma, this was the only way I saw how I could've hurt daddy; make his mouth water over my sexy well-cared-for body, knowing he couldn't touch.

Momma and my brothers were proud of me and delighted with my gifts. I showed them all a picture of me and David in bathing suits leaning against his Benz. Daddy's lips trembled when he looked at it, and I told him to take it – Momma put it on her dresser, right where it would haunt Daddy. Very good.

I told them David was married, and described my apartment. Momma wasn't shocked, since the man was rich and treating me well.

I had forgiven momma for mistreating me. After all, she was my momma and had mistreated me only once, and, then, only because she was too simple-minded a person to have realized that daddy was an evil man.

Throughout my stay I lounged about the yard, or went with daddy and the boys to the bush; in brief and tight shorts, tube tops, mini-skirts and thin blouses. Hair always neat, lipstick or

gloss always fresh and my nails always bright. It was clear to me that he was suffering, since he wanted me but knew if he asked I would snub him. Worse, he had to hide his desire from Momma. I rarely addressed him personally and when I did it was with an air of boredom.

He was all nerves when left alone with me in a room. And whenever it seemed likely that we would end up alone at home, he fled.

Before I left I visited a few old friends. They were all in awe of me.

David and his family were supposed to fly home on the first day of the year. But instead his dead body came home on the 4th. He had died in a car accident on a Canadian highway, on the last day of 1980. His family had not been hurt badly.

David's death hit me very hard. I cried a lot. I had become his mistress because he was rich and generous, but I had grown to truly care for him. I was sure I would never again get so close to almost being in love.

Much as I wanted to I didn't go to David's funeral, because I didn't want to upset his family, whom I was sure knew all about me. I allowed myself to grieve for a month, then began to plot my future.

Tracy wanted me to return to her home. But I didn't, since I knew I would again leave as soon as I found another man. And I intended to find a man very soon.

I cared for Tracy too much to use her as a rung on my climb to the top. I now knew she was madly in love with me as a person, but I also knew I could never even come close to being in love with a woman.

Towards the end of January, the rent collector came to see me. He was a tall, thick, jet-black man of about thirty.

"I know you was the boss' mistress," he said evenly. "But from now on you will have to pay your rent. The wife, Mrs Chin, hired

a manager to run the business. So, " he shrugged, "you'll have to pay up."

"Thank you. How much is the rent?"

"Nine hundred dollars."

"I will stay on," I said. He left.

I had $43,000 in my bank account. If I had been a braver gambler I would've had over $100,000. Even when David had given me what he called 'sure wins', I had refrained from heavy bets.

What would most girls my age do with $43,000? Buy a house or a car? But I intended to use it to make more money. And, of course, I was sure I'd soon hook another rich man.

I thought of investing my money in a retail business. But I decided to return to the track (wasn't I the belle?) and squeeze another $40,000 out of one or two of the 'Kings' by way of being a paramour and getting tips on 'sure wins'. Then I would be able to begin a good business. There was no doubt in my mind that several of the Kings would compete for the honour of having me as their mistress.

Get back to the track, 'La Belle'.

On the first Wednesday in February, 1981, I paid the track my first visit of the year. I went by taxi. Knowing I wouldn't be able to go directly to the VIP box, I went early and hung around the VIP car park knowing I would see the 'Kings' there. I didn't have to wait long. One of the them saw me before he parked his car and he was alone. He parked and hurried towards me. Then after voicing his regret at David's death, he asked me to be his date. I accepted.

First we went to see his horses and trainer. Then we went to the VIP box.

I was stunning and my escort, Calvin, thought so. I was wearing a white sun-hat; white off-the-shoulder lace blouse; narrow knee-length blue skirt with a slit to mid-thigh; grey patterned stockings; white gloves; and blue high-heeled shoes.

134

When Calvin and I entered the box it was clear that every man there envied him. Why, wasn't the man who was responsible for the Belle's return honoured man?

Mr Calvin Dewitt became my new man. He was a tall, blue-eyed, fifty-eight-year-old Jamaican white with greying, curly, dark brown hair. His fleshy frame was still erect and he was agile in bed. He was married and had four children, two boys and two girls, the youngest being a twenty-two-year-old girl.

"You," he often said, "aren't only my mistress but also my third, and only black, daughter."

"Which," I always responded, "makes you guilty of incest."

"Ah, my child. But what pleasure our sins give my old body!"

Calvin was the Chairman of the Dewitt Group of Companies and an enthusiastic race horse owner. He was generous to me, money, gifts and betting tips. He wasn't able to spend as much time with me as David had.

Mrs Dewitt was a jealous fifty-four-year-old white American who had very little interest in horses, but was a tireless social worker. It seemed, from what Calvin told me, she was always murmuring about his infidelity but only got really angry when the grapevine told her that the present mistress had been with Calvin for a year. Then she would scream, shriek and hurl objects at Calvin until he got rid of his 'one-year-old mistress'.

"But," Calvin said, "I am not going to give you up till I die. This time even if she calls in the American Marines I won't be ending our affair after a year. No way."

Thus Calvin and I were free to be bold at the track, where I also met his two sons (they were pleasant to me); the daughters were in the USA.

However, my affair with Calvin lasted for only three months. He died of a heart attack in his office.

After Calvin's death I was shunned by the Kings of the track. A superstitious lot, they saw me as a jinx.

So I stopped going to the track. And, for unknown reasons, I

suddenly became a reckless and compulsive race horse gambler. I just couldn't stop myself from going to the betting shops on race days. And I just couldn't find a rich man who wanted a mistress. Or at least they didn't want me.

Nineteen eighty-one ended; 1982 began. And my savings were going fast. By September 1982, I had only $15,000. And as suddenly as it had come, my compulsion went. I stopped gambling.

Then I remembered a statement David had uttered more than once, "To make money from marijuana, you buy in December to early February when it is plenty and cheap. Then you sell in July to September when it is always scarce. But don't ever buy before mid-December because it may spoil before July."

That was it! My way to riches! Since Calvin's death it didn't seem to make sense to depend on milking rich men. All those I had bedded since then only saw me as a good lay, which they could get all over town for a few dollars. My luck had run out.

The more I thought about the marijuana business the better it seemed. David had taken me to meet planters in St. Catherine and Westmoreland, I was sure they would remember me when I went to see them at the end of the year, four more months to go. But I had to find a job immediately so that I could continue to pay my rent and eat without using anymore of my savings. My apartment (same one David had given, or rather lent, me), I mused, was just right for storing marijuana. All the tenants, except me, were law-abiding citizens who minded their own business.

I decided to become a go-go dancer. Except for whoring, go-go dancing was the only job I was qualified for which could pay my rent.

Tracy was appalled when I told her I was going to be a go-go – I didn't tell her about my plan to become a smuggler, because I knew she would've offered to lend me money; I was determined not to take any more financial help from her; to take more aid from her would've softened my resolve not to return to live at her house; we were still lovers and now that I didn't have a man she was trying her best to get me to move back in with her.

It proved very easy for me to find a job as a dancer. I chose one of the better clubs on Red Hills Road.

I was still having my recurring dream about Carl, and still dismissing it as nonsense. And I had forgotten about my muddled emotions towards him. Someday, I was sure, I was going to hurt him, the Douglases and the male members of the Trigger Squad.

Chapter 23

I was sweating and various muscles were reminding me they weren't used to such work. But it wasn't only sweating that had made the crotch of my white bikini wet. I was aroused sexually, cunt soaking wet, slit throbbing.

It felt damn good to be up on the small stage grinding to music, while all those eyes were feasting on my bikini-clad body under the spotlights which kept changing through a series of colours – now my white bikini had a mixed tint, then tinted red, blue, green, now yellow, then its natural white.

It was my first night as a go-go dancer, and I was an instant hit with this thick Friday night crowd. Those men who weren't shouting had desire written on their faces in the dimly lighted club: no doubt most of their female escorts were irritated.

When my act ended the men shouted and whistled for more. I was tired but was able to grind my way through another record. Then I fled from the stage leaving them clamouring for more. The girl who was going on stage glared at me as I passed her by: obviously the first act of my first night had been too successful for her liking.

I hurried to the small dressing room I had been given. I put on my robe and flopped down onto the divan, exhausted. Too tired to even use a towel. The small divan, a small dressing table and a stool took up most of the room. There was a full-length mirror on the back of the door, walls were painted yellow, a worn green carpet on the floor and dirty white curtains at the small window.

About forty-five minutes later, the short portly owner entered my dreary dressing room. There was a wide grin on his roundish, brown face. He looked just as one expected night club owners/managers to look.

"I can't believe this is your first time as a dancer."

I shrugged. "It is. Perhaps I was born for it."

138

"You were really great," he said earnestly. "It will soon be your turn again. Tired?"

"Slightly. I'll manage."

"You'll soon get used to it." He left.

I got up and refreshed my make-up, changed into a pale yellow bikini and went to the bathroom. Then I went to stand in the wings watching the girl on stage. (There were six of us dancers at El Hombre Club, all between ages eighteen to thirty.)

El Hombre had been one of the most popular night clubs in Kingston, since the late sixties. Expensive but comfortable. The patrons were a colourful mixture of rich and middle-class men. Red Hills Road is internationally renowned as a night club spot, and El Hombre is the best on Red Hills Road. Even though, since '79 to '81, there have been several first class clubs in New Kingston that are frequented by the rich, El Hombre still held its own as one of the very best.

Each dancer at El Hombre had her own tiny dressing room, but we shared a common bathroom. We began dancing at 9:00 p.m. and continued until 3:00 to 4:00 a.m. doing bouts of fifteen minutes on stage. We danced on Friday, Saturday, Sunday, Monday and Tuesday nights – Wednesday nights were band music night and Thursday nights were 'Oldies' party night. There were four waitresses and barmaids who wore different coloured shorts and matching tank top each night. And there were two burly bouncers who wore green three-piece suits.

The club occupied the upper floor of a wide two-storey building. The club room was large with a high ceiling and tall windows and a door led to a long balcony which overlooked the road. There was a long wooden top bar and cushioned stools along one wall; cushioned seats at the base of the semi-circular stage; and small square tables with cushioned chairs on the rest of the floor. There was a small glass booth that housed the music-playing equipment – records and tapes; the music flowed from hidden speakers.

My second round of dancing was as successful as the first had been, but this time I didn't give the encore they roared for. I was so beat I didn't think I could manage another round, but when I went on again the whistlers, cat calls and hungry faces and the spotlights gave me energy to come through – the same thing happened with the other two rounds which completed my first night.

Half an hour after my final round, the owner/manager came to my dressing room. "Carlene," he coaxed, " you can make extra money each night. Right now there are four men offering $100 each for twenty minutes with you."

"No man," I said simply, "can pay me to ball him. But though I am tired I have never felt hornier, my pussy could do with a good wetting. So tell all four to come and you keep all the money."

"You want none of the money?" He was staring incredulously. "I do a 50-50 deal with the others."

"My pussy is priceless. Whenever any of the customers wants me, and I agree, you charge them and take it all."

He left. A minute later the first came.

After I had decided to become a go-go dancer the first place I went to was El Hombre. It had been one of David's favourite clubs, he had known and introduced me to the owner/manager, Mr Black. Then after I had left the 'Kings of the Track' set, El Hombre was one of the clubs I frequented in search of a rich man who needed a young mistress: each of these times I went there, Mr Black sat with me for a while and we had sex a few times.

Mr Black was one of those virile bachelors who was terribly afraid of being attached to a woman; the type who saw himself as a holy phallus for the good of all womankind, God's gift to us lustful females. He had several children, and, to keep the mothers from getting hold of him via the children, he had forced the mothers to allow him to 'farm out' the children to his sisters and aunts.

It had been shortly after dusk on a Monday when I had gone to El Hombre to ask Mr Black for a job as dancer. He asked me to

dance in his small and dull office. A minute after I began he had exclaimed, "Yes! You'll do. Two nights ago I fired one of my girls. Where did you learn to dance?"

"I learned by watching dancers. The only dancing I ever did was for David in my apartment."

"Really? You weren't a dancer before you met David?"

"Why should I lie that I have no real experience?"

"True. And I value honesty. And I am glad to be able to help you. Well, we'll soon know how good you are on stage."

"I'll be good. I love to have men staring at me. The more the better."

"That's an asset." He smiled and ran his eyes over my body; I was only in shoes and bikini underwear. "You sure are something to stare at. When can you begin?"

"Friday."

"Sometime you'll have to dance without a bra. Do you mind?"

"No, I love to tease."

"I know. How about a quick one before you go?"

"Sure." I began to take off my panties.

Mr Black was from a marijuana planting community in St. Ann. He was twenty-five when he had moved to Kingston twenty years ago and began a marijuana retail business with the marijuana he had planted in 1961. He flourished and bought a few taxis in '62. Then in '66 he opened El Hombre, and began to export large quantities of marijuana. Now he was very wealthy and powerful.

As a dancer I was earning $60 a night. Enough to pay my bills now that I had stopped gambling and going to expensive restaurants. After a few weeks the job became less tiring and it was obvious that I was one of the favourite dancers with the customers. Every man, and quite a few women, who came there were willing to pay to screw me. Whenever I felt the urge to get laid by men or women I allowed Mr Black to charge and send them to my dressing room. Mr Black didn't mention, and I wasn't interested to

know, how much money he was earning from my cunt. Occasionally he gave me gifts of expensive perfumes and paintings by the best local artists (slowly my living and dining rooms began to look like an art gallery).

It wasn't long before the other dancers warmed to me and we became friends. They were all bisexuals and occasionally I allowed each to make love to me but because I would soon be a smuggler and would be storing hundreds of pounds of marijuana in my apartment, I didn't want any of them to become too attached to me, and it was for this same reason that I stopped bringing men to my apartment.

Two days before Christmas I rented a Toyota car and went to Westmoreland to see Ras Ipa. I took along $10,000. The reason I intended to spend most of my money with Ras Ipa was that he specialized in producing Sensimilla, seedless or almost seedless marijuana, which was the most sought-after type.

Chapter 24

Ras Ipa lived in a four-bedroom bungalow in the hilly and rocky district of Town Head. He was tall, muscular and black with a pleasant, bearded face. He was thirty-five years old and his thick locks flowed down to near his waist.

Ras Ipa was at home when I arrived after my long, slow drive. I had left Kingston at 5:00 a.m. and parked in Ras Ipa's driveway at 11:20 a.m., behind his battered Ford pick-up van in the carport. Before today, I had not driven for more than fifteen miles, now I had just done over a hundred. But because I had done it at a slow pace I wasn't exhausted.

The mongrel dogs were barking and jumping around my car. Ras Ipa and one of his many children came out onto the verandah. He recognized me immediately.

"Just yesterday," he said, after chasing the dogs, "I man was thinking about yu." He sighed sadly. "Anytime I 'member Mr Chin I 'member yu too. Is him who help to set I man off to a good start in the business. A good man."

"I still miss him a lot." I sighed histrionically. Then looked away as if I were fighting back tears. I got out of the car and turned to look across the valley: Ras Ipa's house was above the road. Below the road the land fell sharply to a stream not far below, beyond which were cultivatęd hillocks (yams and vegetables); behind the house was a wide grassy hillock which gave way to the steep and wooded sloped of the mountains where Ras Ipa and his fellow marijuana planters had their marijuana fields.

"So what," he said, "yu going into business?"

"Yes," I smiled sexily, noting the light in his eyes.

"Wonder if I man remember yu name right. Carlene?"

"Yea. Your memory is good." I was being provocative, fluttering my lashes, leaning against my car like one of those models in car ads. It was my intention to do all I could to get the best bargain from him. That's why I had worn my tight knee-length skirt,

a cotton blouse without bra and no make-up, in case he was one of those rasta men who disliked women in pants and make-up.

He led me to his storeroom at the back of the house. On the way we met his fat and ever smiling wife with about four more of their children. Her face told you she was totally resigned to the problems of this world. "All in Jah hands," I could imagine her saying with fat hands spread wide as she saw visions of Zion.

There were many metal drums in Ras Ipa's store room, and several large heaps of unstripped marijuana bundles on pieces of canvas. It was an unpainted room about twenty feet by fourteen.

"How much per pound?" I asked. We were alone in the room, windows half-closed, door closed.

"The lowest I selling now is $60 a pound. But fo' yu I can go down a bit depending on how much money you hav'." He moved his eyes to my front then back to my face.

Seeing the desire in his red eyes I glanced at his pants front and saw that he was already stiff. "I have $10,000." I smiled into his eyes. "And something special for you. But you will have to lock the door."

He grinned, went to peep through the windows then used his keys to lock the door. "We hav' to be quick," he grinned wickedly. "If my wife catch us she wouldn't raise a fuss or hate yu'. She would quote scriptures to me fo' weeks, would be glad fo' the chance to be free to preach Jah word to me."

I made him sit on one of the two chairs in the room, and gave him a delicate blow-job.

"Jah sons!" he exclaimed softly afterwards. "Girl yu know how to use yu tongue." He sighed contentedly. "Someday I going get to fuck yu."

"I will be dreaming about it."

Ras Ipa gave me 215 pounds of sensimilla. I had brought a large shipping barrel but it could only hold almost two-thirds. Ras Ipa gave me a small shipping barrel which held the rest. "When yu reach home," he advised me, "if yu keep the stuff in these same barrels in a cook room, it will keep fo' years, 'cause I man no use fertilizer."

Just then a group of teenaged girls came to strip the unstripped marijuana on the canvases. Each girl had a small and very sharp knife, which, like their fingers, was black with marijuana gum because they had been stripping marijuana for another planter since daybreak.

I put the larger barrel in my car trunk and the other on the back seat. Ras Ipa agreed with me that the small barrel on my back seat wouldn't look strange, especially since at Christmas time people got barrels from relatives abroad. Plus I was confident that any policeman I met on the way would notice me, not my barrel.

Before I left Ras Ipa's house at shortly before 1:00 p.m. I applied make-up and expensive perfume. The sun was hidden behind grey clouds when I drove away.

On my way to and from Westmoreland I passed through Ewarton, the small town in St. Catherine where I intended to buy some of the cheaper seedy marijuana – termed 'Commercial' – in January from a lusty and odd character known as John Wayne.

Now on my way from Westmoreland I passed through Ewarton at dusk and saw John Wayne outside a bar with two very young girls – about thirteen years old – in his arms. I didn't stop. I was driving at moderate speed, being overtaken regularly by merry Christmas drivers. Having told Mr Black it was unlikely that I would turn up for work that night, I had no need to hurry.

I was on the Spanish Town Highway when a police patrol car pulled up beside me on the inside lane. The uniformed police men signalled me to stop. Fear gripped me for a moment but I quickly withheld it from turning to panic. I pulled over onto the road shoulder. The cops stopped several yards behind me.

Carlene, I remonstrated with myself, fear is your greatest enemy now, charm your best friend.

We had stopped near one of the brilliant sodium lamps that lit most of the highway. There were canefields on both sides of the highway. The moon wasn't up yet but the clear sky was lit by stars, and a caressing Christmas breeze was blowing. It was just after

145

7:00 p.m. and the highway was fairly busy, all in the spirit of the merry season.

Via my rear view and outside mirrors I saw that the policeman coming towards me was young. Carlene, I told myself, no matter what these two cops are up to you can use your charm to set it all right, even if you have to ball them here on the well-lit highway. This thought calmed me a bit.

"Goodnight, Miss." He was tall, good looking and very black. I flashed my Bo Derek smile, "Good night, officer."

Desire made him lick his lips before saying, "One of your back wheels seemed wobbly, that's why we stopped you."

I used mock alarm to hide my relief. Then I realized that a wobbly wheel could be very serious and I became sincerely alarmed. "Thank God you saw it! And it's very sweet of you to have stopped me." I reached out and squeezed one of his hands. He blushed, cleared his throat and said, "My duty as an officer and a fellow human. My colleague is coming with our lug tool."

I got out of the car swaying my hips like Pam Grier, a sexily aggressive sway. "You must give me your names so I can report your kindness."

"No need for that, miss." He was having a hard time keeping his eyes off me.

"I insist. Citizens should report the good deeds you men do. That will help your superiors to know who to promote."

Just then his colleague came up with the lug tool. He was short, fleshy and looked near thirty.

I turned towards the newcomer. "I was just saying I should report this act of kindness which shows you are observant and dedicated. " I paused dramatically. "Plus my dad has lots of friends among the commanding officers of the force."

Their faces lit up. "I am Lance Corporal Smith," the short one said. "He is Constable Brown. We are from Ferry Station."

They tightened the nuts on the wobbly wheel and checked the others.

"Thanks a million." I beamed. "You probably saved my life. Have a happy holiday."

"Glad to have helped!"
"Merry Christmas!"
I got in my car and drove away. Well, I thought, let that be a lesson. Policemen do more than hunt lawbreakers and search cars. Don't ever panic when you have marijuana and policemen stop you. And like all men they can be blinded by beauty and charm. They say that even gay men enjoy gazing at a beautiful woman.

When I arrived at my apartment building I asked the night watchman to help me move my barrels to the elevator. I tipped him generously, and I was sure he didn't suspect that my barrels didn't contain gifts from relatives abroad – the barrels looked new and were shut so tight not a whiff of marijuana scent could've escaped; plus, the watchman was middle-aged and obviously was only concerned with his job.

My barrels and I went up alone in the elevator, and we met nobody in the corridor. It was easy going for me to roll them the short distance from the elevator to my apartment. I then took a nap, showered and ate a few sandwiches and milk. I felt so good I drove to the club and began working at 11:00 p.m., fifteen minutes after I had arrived. I was so horny by the time I did my last bout at 3:00 a.m. that I had to call for two men at once and had them together twice – sucked each once and was fucked by each once. Then I had two others singly.

I was glad that all the men in my apartment building went to New Kingston night clubs. I was friendly with none of them and was polite to their wives and common-law loves. I supposed that most of them thought I was now some sort of whore but tolerated me because it was obvious I didn't use my apartment as my entertainment spot. A few of the women invited me to Christmas parties, which I attended and left at midnight. None of them would've suspected I was a smuggler. To them I was an unskilled young·woman who had lost her wealthy lover and was now a whore or worked with an escort service company.

147

On the second Wednesday afternoon in 1983, I drove another rented car to Martin's Bush, Ewarton. John Wayne wasn't at home. I opened his gate and drove into his flat, dusty, grassless front yard. His house was a small bungalow. The afternoon was still and hot, the sun just about to dip behind the mountains in the west. From where I was, I could see several distant marijuana fields on the front slopes of the mountains.

Ewarton is situated at the foot of three mountain ranges, each on one side of the town, the fourth side of the town is the extension of the narrow valley where Linstead and Bog Walk are also situated.

John Wayne's parents lived next door to him. Shortly his mother came over and told me he was in the hills and most likely would not be returning before dusk. She said she could sell me some marijuana. I told her I would wait until John Wayne came home. It did seem funny that a lady over sixty with Bible in hand was offering to sell me marijuana. I followed her to her house and sat on the verandah. Shortly a mass of school children came through the gate; I knew some of them belonged to John Wayne, the rest were his nephews and nieces.

When John Wayne came home at dusk he was pleased to see me. And I was pleased to find he had not changed his lifestyle since the last time I had seen him almost three and half years ago. He still had no special woman. And though he wasn't yet thirty he had a dozen children with as many girls: It seemed he thought he had been born to populate the earth. He had been planting his own marijuana field since age fourteen. He was called John Wayne because only cowboy movies interested him (especially those with John Wayne), and he only read novels of the 'wild west'.

Two of his workers accompanied him with two bags of marijuana. "I sorry Mr Chin dead," he said solemnly. "A feel it. Still a glad to see yu." He was big, black and clean-shaven with close cropped hair.

We went into his scantily furnished, slightly untidy but clean two-bedroom house.

"I have $5,000," I said. "My savings. I want some stuff and will spend the night if you want me."

"Ah," he grinned. We were in the sofa in his well-lit living-room. "I want you to stay the night. Let I go bathe, then eat what my mother leave fo' me and we'll go on the town fo' a bit. Did momma feed yu?"

"Yea."

"We'll hav' a late supper out on the town. When we come home a show yu what a real stallion can do."

"You might be surprised what this little filly can do."

He guffawed. "I like that. Me a stallion, yu a filly. Great! But be warned I am famous for making babies."

"Mmm, might be interesting to have one for you."

He grinned and left.

After taking a bath he put on jeans, a brown shirt, brown cow-boy-style boots and a brown broad brimmed felt hat. I changed my blouse (I had an overnight bag) and repaired my make-up; I wore jeans and sandals. He suggested we ride his Honda 750 into town, but I insisted we go in my rented car. He didn't own a car, he said, because he didn't like driving. He saw bikes as the next best thing to a horse.

We drove to the small, one street commercial centre of Ewarton that was at the very foot of Mount Diablo. We spent an hour at the leading club which was very crowded for a mid-week night. John Wayne explained that it was because it was harvest time and everyone had marijuana to sell and buyers had been about aplenty since recently.

After the club we went to a restaurant and had jerked chicken with fried rice, drank a few beers and then returned to his house.

He had a huge cock and knew how to use it.

We awoke just before dawn next morning. "Yu damn good fo' a young girl," he said.

"You are a hell of a man."

"A stallion."

"Yea," I giggled. "A thoroughbred."

149

We got out of bed. I wanted to be on the road early. He wanted to reach his marijuana field early. While I showered and dressed he packed 160 pounds of marijuana into the large shipping barrel I had brought. Then he fixed me a light breakfast.

The sun was just up when I drove away. I saw several groups of marijuana planters heading for the hills – some were dressed as if on their way to an office.

I thought it best not to go by way of Spanish Town, since I might meet L/C Smith and Constable Brown and arouse their suspicion. I drove the long way around, via St Mary. It was a pleasant fate awaiting me a journey's end.

Chapter 25

I arrived in Kingston without being stopped by the law. It was near 10:30 a.m. when I parked in the near-empty parking lot in front of my apartment building. I felt stiff as I got out of the car. Then a man got out of a nearby car and turned towards me.

It was Carl Bell, dressed casually.

My heart expanded, my pulse raced and my stomach quivered. He smiled and with a few long confident strides he was by my side. I felt oddly weak and had to lean on my car.

"Hello, Carlene. I just had to see you. So I decided to sit here in my car all day if necessary. I intend to keep my promise not to come to your door...until I am invited."

I had thought that by now all feelings except my desire for revenge for him, would be dead, both those of body and mind. But to my dismay a warmth began in the core of my being and rapidly spread all over my body. 'How could you,' my mind screamed, 'want to hurt a man who stirred you so easily, even though he did hurt you once.' Unable to move my eyes from his searching gaze, our eyes remained locked for what seemed like a lifetime, the silence weighed down my magnetism.

"Hello Carl." My voice was unsteady and the words were not of my control.

He ran his eyes over me, causing my clit to hum. My breasts were on show through the thin T-shirt and my white pants clung to me like a second skin. When his eyes came back to my face they were cloudy and I gulped half the atmosphere. What was wrong with me? How come this man, my enemy, affected me so?

"I saw you," he suddenly beamed, "dancing Monday night," (I hung my head; Ashamed? Why?), "and you were very good. I don't really disapprove." His manner was now 'a serious big brother'. "But you were not a dancer when we last met. So I had to see you to find out how things were with you. I must confess that I have been keeping an eye on you to prevent you from moving without me knowing." (Indignation flared up in me!) He saw my

151

anger and continued hurriedly. "You have no family in Kingston and I do feel indebted to you," (my anger subsided as quickly as it had flared up) "and also duty-bound to protect."

"Thanks," I heard myself whisper, eyes downcast. "My man died in January '81 and now I need money but I'm not qualified for a good office job." Why was I telling him this? Feeling confused, I glared at him and said defiantly, "I won't go back to being a helper. And I would rather die than be a whore."

"I wouldn't want you to." His voice was warm, smile and eyes showing relief, as if he was proud of me. He gripped my shoulders, causing me to burn with uncontrollable ecstasy. "Carlene, you did right. Dancing is like modeling."

Totally bewildered and wanting him, I was forced to say, "Help me carry my barrel up to my apartment."

He removed the barrel from my car trunk – it was a new and well-sealed barrel. In silence we carried it into the lobby, then into the elevator with two housewives coming from the pool. He was wearing jeans and sport shirt but I knew the women saw that he was a decent and very educated young man. And I was glad they distracted my jumbled thoughts and my passion by saying a few words to me. I introduced them to Carl. However, the ladies left two floors before mine, and by the time Carl and I got out of the elevator I was once more overwhelmed by desire for him. I had stopped trying to fight or understand my feelings. It seemed best to bed him today; doing so, I thought, would be sure to set me straight in mind and body.

When I opened my door and stood aside to let him enter he said, "Sure you want me to enter."

The bastard knew I wanted him. "You deserve a drink," I said huskily.

He rolled the barrel into my apartment. Are you mad, I thought, imagine you are about to bed a man you hate? Get rid of him!

But it was too late. He pulled me inside, closed the door and took me in his arms. I melted. Powerless.

"Know what drink I want?" Then he was on his knees and in

no time my pants and panties were below my knees. He began to lick my damp cunt. I began to whimper like a puppy, leaning against the door, legs wide, eyes closed, hands ruffling his low hair. Shortly I climaxed. Then driven by some primitive instinct I pranced on him like a wild animal.

A minute later, we were both naked and we fucked right there on the living room carpet with my paintings and carvings as witnesses to my wild abandon. We achieved a nerve shattering simultaneous climax which shook the earth and my soul.

And I immediately knew our lovemaking wouldn't clear my muddled feelings for him; instead I was more confused. And I was angry at myself for having allowed my body to betray me. Then he made things worse by saying, "I love you, Carlene."

I leapt to my feet. Why did he have to speak of love when to him I was only a good lay? Did he still see me as a fool? He did think I was stupid.

"You know nothing of love!" I exploded. "I don't love you. Leave and don't come back. What you just got is your pay for bringing up my barrel."

His face flushed and frowned indignantly.

"I would just as quickly lay a dog as you!" I was hopping mad, feet planted wide, hands on hips.

He was now an angry purple. He struggled into his clothes under my strong glare. Then he gulped air, and with searching eyes he asked, "How long will you deny the truth?"

"Get out! I hate you! And someday I am going to get my revenge!"

With one last bewildered look at me, he left slamming the door behind him.

"Beast!" I shrieked and, strangely, I sank to the carpet and wept.

Later after a good sleep, a bath and coffee with a bit of brandy, I allowed myself to think about my confusing reactions to Carl that morning and our previous meeting two and a half years before.

A strange voice whispered the answer. Carl was using some

form of obeah oil to make any woman he chose be his slave.

That was it! The bastard!

Obeah oil, I concluded, was the only rational explanation why a sane young woman would be drawn to a man she despised. After all, he had not had such a power over my will when I was at his house. Oh, someday I was going to make him pay.

Having solved the riddle of my torn emotions, I was able to regain full control of my wits. Would he try to subdue me again? Should I go seek counsel with an obeah worker? But, I mused, I knew nothing about such people but I knew there were many false ones who only wanted to earn an easy living.

'Wait,' I thought, 'and see if he is going to come molest you again. And now that I know his secret I might be able to withstand the power of his obeah oil.'

I kept two of my marijuana barrels in my bathroom, the other in my bedroom. I had no urge to smoke and didn't, even when Tracy sampled each kind and told me they were good. She and two of my fellow dancers were the only visitors to my apartment; but Tracy was the only person who knew I had marijuana in the barrels.

The months passed. I didn't see Carl, and though I was still having the recurring dream about him and me at sea, I rarely remembered him. When I did think of him it was to ponder how and when I would be able to get my revenge against him. And I now knew the recurring dream was a symbol of the depth of my hatred for him.

June ended. Marijuana was in short supply. Mr Black and Tracy helped me find customers. I rented a different car every week, and for five weeks I was driving about town everyday from noon to 7:00 p.m. delivering marijuana. I sold no less than a pound and as much as twenty pounds to each person.

I made a profit of fifty thousand dollars.

The thought of extracting money from men became a thing of the past. All I needed them for was sexual ease when, and only

when, I so desired – they were just like so many tins of oil a car needed to go on; and at times I wished I could live without the thrill of having a man spill his seed in my cunt. I was now a smuggler who bought in December to January and sold in July to August. I decided to continue dancing because it would keep me from spending my savings of $68,000; dancing would act as a front; and I needed some form of work to keep me tuned – and I did enjoy dancing.

Tracy and I 'went out on the town' one Thursday night to celebrate my good fortune. We had a seven course dinner at one of the best restaurants in town, drank two bottles of their best champagne. Then we went to the best New Kingston disco and flirted with several men, leaving them panting with lust at midnight and went to my apartment where we had a ball in bed.

We awoke at 11:00 a.m. next morning. After breakfast Tracy said, "I have closed my business. I want you to come live with me and help set up a chic ladies' boutique. We'll go to New York, Paris, London, Rome, Milan and select the best to open our shop. We'll be a hit."

She was excited. I disliked having to disappoint her but I had to tell her the truth. "Tracy, I will help with your store, but I will never return to live with you. It wouldn't work..."

She had paled. "My love," she pleaded, "I won't mind you having lovers, male and female. I won't boss you around."

"I know," I said soothingly, she looked so vulnerable. "It's hard to explain. I just have to make it on my own. Buy my own home because someday I might decide to have one or two children even though I won't ever tie myself to any man. But you and I can always be lovers."

"That's not enough." Her voice was small and wistful and I knew she was about to drop a bomb. "The truth is, I am not interested in sex with men anymore. It is as if I have grown into being a complete lesbian. I want you to dominate me, be my rock, my master, my goddess. I'll even bear a child to make our relationship complete." (I was stunned. It was as if she was a stranger to

me; in fact a submissive air had descended round about her.) "Basically," she added in explanation, "I am weak. I need a strong woman who is younger than me.

"You are strong enough to make me feel safe and secure. And I really wouldn't mind you having male lovers. I'll do only what you say. Please give our love a chance."

"No, Tracy," I said sadly. "What you need is a young bull-dyke." For a while she gazed at me. Then seeing it was hopeless, she got up and left without another word. It was over between us.

Several months later I heard that a new boutique called *Tracy's* was having a glamourous opening. I went there four days after the opening. Sure enough, it was my old friend and lover, Tracy. She looked completely different – shy, submissive, girlish. She introduced me to a tall, lean, flat-chested and tough-looking Texan girl who seemed no more than twenty years old and had close cropped brown hair and green eyes. Obviously, the Texan was her dyke-husband.

I began to seriously think of taking some action against the male members of the Trigger Squad. This was due to more than a desire for revenge; it was becoming tiresome to have to be always looking for them and being afraid to shop in the Half-Way-Tree area. There was no doubt in my mind they would want to hurt me whenever we met. And the only way it seemed I could remove the threat of them hurting me was to kill them. ¨Pay to have them murdered.

One of my dancing colleagues, Marie, had a brother who was a policeman. Occasionally, this policeman and his best friend, also a cop, came to the club. Marie had introduced them to me and it was obvious they were a bit shy for their ages, twenty and nineteen. I decided they could be useful in my need to eliminate the Squad. So one night in September, I asked them to escort me home.

I had not had any men before I had left the club, so as soon as

we arrived at my apartment I made it clear I wanted them both.

Within a week I had enslaved them to the point where the three of us began to sleep together. Whenever they weren't on duty they were with me, so much that I rarely allowed Mr Black to send men to me at the club, though my two worshippers didn't mind me bedding other men at the club and knew they were the only men I took to my apartment. The elaborate meals I cooked them made our three-some more official.

Within three weeks my two law-men would have shot the Prime Minister if I had told them to. I was the fulfillment of their sexual fantasies, their Venus, queen and teacher in one. Before long everyone at the club was calling us 'Queen Carlene and her Knights'.

In November, I told them the truth about me and my step daddy and Kevin and the Squad. Immediately they went on the war path.

They soon found out that three of the squad had been killed in the political violence of 1980 and the others had migrated to the United States where they were involved in drugs and gun running.

I was free of the Squad.

And soon my life was to take on a new dimension.

Chapter 26

Near the end of the year my two law-men were invited to the USA to join a drug ring which was being led by one of their childhood friends. They accepted the offer, since it promised quick wealth. But they vowed that they would never stop loving me and intended to return to me if I wouldn't join them in the United States – their friend could issue U.S. visas as if he were an embassy.

"But, my loves," I protested with a sexy pout, "I am sure you both hope to marry and raise families. Every man should." We were in bed after a wild daytime bout.

"We have discussed it," the older one said, "and would be willing to share you and any children you had. If you agree."

I was stunned, dumb, incredulous. Was I hearing right? Was I dreaming?

"For us to marry," commented the younger, "it would mean one of us would have to go search for a woman like you. And I doubt if there is or ever was anyone like you."

"No, no, my darlings" I said maternally. "What would we tell our kids?"

"The truth."

"Yeah. The truth."

"It wouldn't," I said sweetly, "work in this world. What you are both going to do is find nice, young wives, and if any of you ever goes with another woman, excepting me, I will help your wives break your hands. Now come make love to your lady who'll always be available." I grasped their cocks.

In the last week of November I rented a three-bedroom house in Liguanea and moved from my apartment. Before my two lawmen left the island in January 1984 they helped transport $45,000 worth of marijuana in a mini removal van – 430 pounds from Ras Ipa, 470 pounds from John Wayne. I stored the marijuana in nine shipping barrels in the bedroom which was unfurnished: The rest of my new home was furnished modestly but comfortably. The

house was surrounded by a small grassy yard with two cherry trees in the backyard. The hibiscus fence was high and thick. The rooms were spacious and newly painted, and the bathrooms and kitchen in good condition. It was a bungalow with the master bedroom and its bathroom and the small kitchen to one side of the living-dining room; the other two bedrooms, a tiny bathroom and carport to the other side; and the small verandah between carport and master bedroom. The community was a middle-class area of bungalows.

At the beginning of February I rented a car and went to the country for my older brother, who was now near eighteen, and his girlfriend, who was eighteen. I spent a night in the country and was pleased to see that momma and daddy seemed happier then ever.

Mr Black gave my brother a job in the supermarket which was below El Hombre. My brother's girl, Lorna, cooked and kept the house and washed my clothes.

Mr Black was delighted that my two law-men lovers were gone. Once again I was getting all my cocks at the club and he was charging them all.

Except for Mr Black I didn't take any men to my home. But I often invited my dancing colleagues and the occasional school girl I sometimes seduced.

It took my brother and Lorna quite a while to accept my bisexuality.

Marijuana was so scarce in the summer of '84 that when I began selling at the beginning of July I could ask for a sky-high price. Once again my sales method was to drive around delivering packages of one to twenty pounds to selected customers. When I was sold out at the end of August, I had made a whopping profit of $137,000.

For the next few years, I kept increasing my investment and my profit kept soaring.

In November 1984, Mr Black helped me to get a good second

hand Mazda car for a very reasonable price from one of his friends who was a wealthy smuggler and owed much of his success to Mr Black. So I was twenty-four, single and on my way to the top.

It was now one year since I had moved into my Liguanea home. But I had only exchanged polite greetings with my next door neighbours. I wasn't worried about what they thought of me. They had no reason to suspect I was a smuggler and my landlord was a police inspector who was Mr Black's friend.

My brother and his girlfriend and I went to spend Christmas Eve day, Christmas and Boxing Days in the country. Like on my former visit ten months ago, I was happy that daddy's eyes held no fear or lust when he looked at me. I saw only paternal pride mixed with repentance when he looked at me regardless of how scanty my clothing was. And he and momma seemed happier than ever. His eyes followed her as if he had just fallen in love with her. Clearly she was now the centre of his world.

On Boxing Day I made sure daddy and I were alone for a while. "Daddy," I said, "I want you to know I have forgiven you of your sins against me."

Tears filmed his eyes. "You have just made me truly happy. Now I can truly be at peace."

Before leaving I told momma and daddy I was a go-go dancer and smuggler. They said they were glad I wasn't a whore. They saw nothing evil about marijuana and their fears that I might end up in jail were greatly relieved when I told them about my good relationship with Mr Black and his powerful contacts in the security forces.

As soon as I returned to Kingston I rented a small moving van and went to see Ras Ipa. His wife and all the younger children were away on a visit to her parents' home, which was about fifteen miles away, leaving only the two oldest children – two boys, aged seventeen and sixteen – with Ras Ipa.

"Yu mus' spend today, tonight and part of tomorrow with I."

His tone was pleading. "I wife not coming back till two day time."

"Won't your sons tell on you?"

"Not if we let them help with yu."

I grinned. "Good idea. It should be fun. I'll stay."

We went to the village's public phone. I phoned my home and told Lorna I wouldn't be home until the following night.

In the afternoon, Ras Ipa fucked me in his storeroom. It was exciting to be fucked amidst drums and bags of marijuana and the strong, fresh scent of the unstripped bundles lying in a large canvas on the middle of the room.

But the night proved much more interesting. Ras Ipa's two sons wore their hair in locks which was short because they had only stopped combing and cutting their hair since leaving school a year and a half ago.

At 7:30 p.m. I retired to the room Ras Ipa had given me. It was a spacious room which held two king-sized beds on which his four daughters slept. Shortly the older of the two boys came in, his head hung shyly.

"Daddy say a mus' come," he whispered. It was clear he was no virgin but was bewildered by his father's action.

"You daddy think it's time you had a real woman," I coaxed. "Ever had a girl older than you?"

"No."

"I undressed and the sight of my curvy body in the bright overhead light made him tear off his clothes. I led him to one of the beds and balled him under the bright lights. He left reluctantly.

As soon as the younger one entered the brightly lit room, a minute later, I knew he was a virgin. This knowledge overwhelmed with a strange and powerful lust. I felt like a drug addict who was starved for a fix. I was being propelled by ecstasy as I strode with long strides toward the young man who was leaning against the closed door gaping with desire and fear.

Without speaking I led him to bed and undressed his trembling body, which was lean and hard. (I was already naked, had not bothered to dress after his brother had left.) His manhood was

only half erect. But as soon as I touched him he became fully erect. I kissed and caressed him all over until my ecstasy was threatening to tear me apart, my breathing heavy, and I saw myself as a goddess whose worshippers had given up the best of their virgin sons to be seduced by me and thereby assure my immortality. Then I straddled him – how else could a goddess take, or rather claim, a boys' virginity?

He didn't last long, but I climaxed noisily as his seed spilled forth in the sacred grounds of my cunt. And I felt as if I had been filled by pure energy, making me feel alive and strong as never before. I had found a new dimension to myself; I now knew I was no ordinary woman; I was a goddess who must be fed by boys' virginity.

I aroused my first victim once more and allowed him to ride on top this time, which was exciting and strengthening but not like the first round.

Ras Ipa and I spent the rest of the night and next morning in bed. I was insatiable, strengthened by the virginity I had claimed.

In the early afternoon I drove out of Ras Ipa's yard with 960 pounds of sensimilla in barrels in the back of my van. Ras Ipa had allowed three of his friends to sell me a total of 600 pounds of the marijuana I had bought; while he had sold me 340 pounds and gave me 20 pounds extra for my sex.

I reached home safely. A new woman. Really a goddess. My new passion for virgin boys overwhelmed me so much I temporarily forgot about my need to get revenge against Mr and Mrs Douglas and Carl.

I began to comb the city for virgin boys.

Chapter 27

I was out of my mind with Olympian ecsatsy. I had just straddled one virgin and was fondling another. It was clear I was about
to have the quickest orgasm of my life.

After my return to Kingston I had began to wonder if the ecstasy I had experienced with Ras Ipa's virgin son, and the strength
his seed had seemed to give me, had been some wild fancy because
I had smoked a marijuana cigar. So I tried and had been able to
suppress my desire for virgin boys for three weeks during which
I had bought 1000 pounds of marijuana from John Wayne and his
friend. But as soon as I had returned from Ewarton I began to
dream of, and yearn for, virgin boys. I couldn't eat and began to feel
weak. It seemed that if I didn't seduce a virgin boy I was gong to
die.

Taking Ras Ipa's son's virginity had made me a goddess who
could only survive by having a steady flow of virgin boys. Perhaps
I was the reincarnation of a queen who had practised such a religious ritual in praise of an ancient god, gods or goddess? Whatever
the source of my desire was, the fact was that I was hooked on virgin boys.

On a sunny Wednesday afternoon I had driven to the Jamaica
College, a high school on Hope Road. Coming down Hope Road,
I neared the school gates just as the first set of boys came pouring
through the gates. They looked lovely in their blue uniform, and
my desire soared. My heart raced, my cunt got damp. I ignored
the older boys, knowing most of them wouldn't be virgins. Then
I saw two of the younger boys standing off by themselves thumb-
ing a ride, and some in-bred (or in-born?) mechanism told me they
were both virgins – that primitive mechanism of mine was never to
fail me.

I pulled alongside my two quarries. "Hello," my voice was
husky. "I can give you boys a lift."

Several other boys rushed up to my car in search of a lift. "Only these two boys," I said firmly. "Nobody else. My shocks are a bit off."

My two quarries got in the backseat. Another boy, who my instinct told me wasn't a virgin, tried to sneak in. "Nobody else," I said firmly glaring at him. He backed off. One of my victims closed the door. I drove off.

Being early afternoon, traffic was thin, but I kept the car at a slow crawl, my blood hot with excitement and desire. "Where do you boys live?"

"Hughenden." He was slim, short, brown and wore plastic framed glasses. The other one was also brown-skinned but he was taller and was beginning to shape-up like a man.

"You boys seem very nice, which is why I gave you a lift." Via the rear view mirror I saw them smile, shy yet proud. Then I added sweetly, "In fact I want you boys to go home now with me and make love with me."

They gaped.

"Don't be alarmed," I said in a cosy soothing voice. "You are special boys, the kind I need to be happy. Don't you think I am sexy?"

They glanced at each other nervously. Had I been too abrupt? Mustn't scare them. Scare them too much and they mightn't be of any use when I got them in bed. "A woman," I said sincerely, "can't be too big for a boy, though a man can be too big for a girl." I paused. "Are you both in the same class."

"Yes, miss." His voice was unsteady.

"My name is Carlene." I was still crawling the car. "What's your names?"

"Dennis." The taller one.

"Robert." The shorter and bespectacled one.

"Lovely names," I cooed, pleased to note they had lost some of their nervousness, "for special boys. Are you related?"

"No miss...Carlene." This from Dennis with a timid smile.

"You may find it hard to believe, but," I lied, "I am only nine-

teen and a half years old." I increased speed, I was badly in need of their virginities, but I also sensed it was best to keep a stream of small talk going. "What class are you boys in? And how old?" "Third form," Dennis said. "I am fifteen." "I am fourteen," Robert said almost defiantly. Good, they were losing their fear. "Age has little," I said, "to do with what a person is worth. There are a lot of adults who are stupid. For example, most big men are coarse and hurt us women in bed. And they think we shouldn't complain. I know you boys are going to be gentle when you grow up. Women are crazy about men who aren't coarse.

"Did you boys see the movie..."

It wasn't a long journey to my home. But I will never be able to understand how, in the face of my intense desire, I was able to keep talking and kept the car on the road. When I did stop the car in the carport my panty was already wet with love-juice and my passionate need overwhelmed me. I propelled my two victims past a surprised Lorna – my brother's girl – to my bedroom. First, I tore off my clothes, and was made even madder by the lustful way my victims gaped at my naked flesh.

I helped my victims undress. The taller one, Dennis, was fully aroused. Robert was semi-erect and seemed nervous once more (my desire was so overwhelming I had forgotten that it would have been better to have left one outside the bedroom). I pushed them both onto my king-sized bed, which had a thick and heavily carved headboard. And without delay I had straddled Dennis and was blindly fondling Robert.

Now, a minute after straddling Dennis, I experienced on Olympian orgasm. Involuntarily, I began to weep. Gratitude. But I continued to rock and sway with Dennis' erect manhood still safely inside me, and I stopped fondling Robert. "Oh you feel so good inside me! Sweet and gentle!" I saw that he wasn't going to last much longer, and the thought and expectation of his seed spilling inside me caused my body to be fired with new ecstasy that soared as fast as a beam of light.

"Fill me with your seed!" I whimpered with Olympian ecstasy. "I...need...it...to...live..."

Then with a groan he began to spill his seed inside my warm playground. I climaxed noisily a second later and could feel new strength beginning to grip my body.

By now Robert was panting with desire. I straddled him. Ecstasy flooded me. He didn't last long. But again as soon as I felt his hot seed begin to spurt I was gripped by the earth-shaking throes of another orgasm.

I had had three orgasms in less than ten minutes!

Feeling contented I lay down and cuddled them both, as I savoured the wondrous feeling of the Olympian strength spreading from my cunt, which was now acting like a stomach, to very section of my body.

"Thank you my loves, you have just given me strength to go on."

I allowed them to fuck me as they wished – which didn't excite me – then made them shower and dress, and gave them a snack. I drove them near to their homes.

As was to be my practice I told them they shouldn't try to visit me. "Now you are to go forth," I said sternly, "and slay school girls. I never bed man or boy twice. So don't take my refusal to see you boys again to be personal."

They were bewildered, but didn't question my will.

I was sure Lorna told my brother about me and the first two school boys I took home, but neither he nor she said anything to me about my new passion, and they continued to refrain from commenting as I began to bring a steady flow of virgin school boys to my bed.

I went in search of virgin boys every two weeks (that was how long I could survive without becoming noticeably weak, spiritually and physically) and I never failed to trap one to woo; when I trapped more than one I took them into my bedroom one at a time. Some weeks I sought preys two or three afternoons. I always got a prey or two by offering them a lift. (Such a good thing I had

bought a car!) And I spread my net to include all schools except for those in West Kingston.

Most of my victims were in the twelve to fifteen age group; I found a few in the sixteen to eighteen age group; that primitive instinct of mine never failed to show me the virgins in any group. I thought it was best not to take on more than three boys at a time, and I mostly limited myself to two.

I knew that, regardless of how careful I was, eventually I would become known as a seducer of boys. But I just couldn't stop: I needed the seeds of virgin boys to keep up my new found strength and to sustain the sacred state of Olympian grace in which I now moved – the act of claiming a boy's virginity always took me through a world of ancient and sacrificial ecstasy to the clouds of the sacramental orgasm which gave me this Olympian grace. And having achieved this divine state, how could I bear the agony of returning to being an ordinary woman?

I took all possible precautions to keep my holy passion a secret for as long as possible. And sometimes, I used rented cars when going in search of victims.

I was still balling men at the nightclub, and Mr Black sometimes spent a day with me. But these were for ordinary sexual satisfaction which I still found enjoyable.

On a Monday afternoon when I was due to claim one or two virgins, I decided to see if one or two boys who weren't virgins would retain my Olympian grace and strength. It turned out that I picked up four boys aged between thirteen and sixteen; four close friends, two of whom were brothers and none of them a virgin. I took them home and balled them all, but the Olympian ecstasy didn't occur and there was nothing divine or sacred about the one orgasm I had.

This proved that I needed virgin boys. The following afternoon I went out and trapped three virgin boys.

Occasionally I came across a boy who was too scared to get it

up no matter what I did. Whenever this happened I dismissed the unworthy victim with a vivid show of my sacred contempt for this sacrilegious behaviour. (Does a goddess or priestess have pity for weaklings? Since my body was a temple, my pússy the sacrificial altar, wasn't it an unforgivable sin for a prey to fail to give up the sacrament of his virginity?) No doubt these few heretical lads were led by my contemptuous words and glares to think I was mad or was a witch.

In the summer of 1985 I made a profit of $520,000 from my marijuana sales. I was surely on my way to great wealth.

When schools had given summer holidays at the end of June I had to change my method of trapping virgin boys. It was easy to pick up my quota at the video games centres, weekend and summer schools.

Then in September when school reopened I came up with the glorious idea which was to make my task of getting sacramental virgin seeds a lot easier and profitable. The idea was to open a club/guardian centre for boys aged ten to sixteen. I found the perfect location for my club and my bank was enthusiastic about my idea especially when Mr Black invested $400,000 for a thirty-three percent share of the business; my bank lent me $800,000 (I had $740,000 in my account.) And I left my go-go job.

The premises I acquired to house my 'Schoolboys' Club' was a large two-storey house on Constant Spring Road. It was surrounded by a half acre of ill-kept grounds and there was a fair-sized swimming pool. I renovated the building; cleaned and landscaped the grounds; extended the swimming pool; put in a badminton, a squash and two lawn tennis courts; a table tennis hall was equipped; and various types of electronic games made available. Chairs, tables and walls were of cheerful colours. And, of course, there was a satellite dish and large televisions in three separate rooms, and a music room with the best records and lots of tapes.

After an intense two-week advertisement drive, we had a grand

opening on the last Saturday of November. It had taken a lot of hard work to get everything ready in only eleven weeks.

The large crowd of middle and upper class parents and children who came to our opening was impressed by our programmes, facilities and our staff of married women, fathers and my charming self. (I was the chairman of the three-person board; Mr Black was the second board member; Mrs Bailey, middle-aged widow and part-time teacher, was the managing director.) We acquired more members at our opening than I had expected.

Our fees ensured that only the upper middle-class and the rich could afford to send their children to our club. Our security measures and our predominantly female staff made parents feel easy about sending their boys to our club. We were open on school days from 2:00 p.m. to 6:30 p.m.; 8:00 a.m. to 7:30 p.m. everyday during the holidays.

We had instructors for lawn tennis, badminton, squash, table tennis and swimming. There was a good cook and a comfortable dining room.

My main task was to move among the boys listening to complaints and requests. I was also head counsellor and their best friend. When my body called for a sacrament of virgin seed I just took a victim to my posh second-storey office which had its own bathroom. Once in my office I immediately led the boy to the divan that was mainly for claiming virginities.

It was known by all that when I went to my office, whether with or without a boy, I was never to be disturbed. All the problems and day-to-day decisions were solely the concern of Mrs Bailey, the managing director.

After claiming a boy's virginity I always used a wash-rag and soap to clean my victim in the bathroom. And I stressed the importance of keeping our coupling a secret, and made it very clear that there wouldn't be a repeat performance. Most of my victims remained in awe of me and showed as much respect as they had before I had claimed their virginity. The few who became too familiar I was always able to cut back down to size with hard looks and a few sharp words.

To keep my love for virgin boys from becoming too open, sometimes for two or three months, I still sought victims at schools, video shops and cinemas. No doubt some of the victims at my club told their friends they had been seduced by me. But since they were all boys I knew there was very little chance of my sacred ritual being told to a parent. Members of my staff eventually got suspicious but were mum on the subject since they all were glad for their jobs and knew I owned 67% of the business.

Mrs Bailey, the managing director, soon found out about my seduction of boys (she, and nobody else, didn't know I only seduced virgins). But I had known her from my days with the Douglases and we – Mrs Bailey and I – were now lovers again and she loved the well-paid job as manager of the club. She was a short, plump, heavy-breasted black woman in her early forties with a round, cheerful face and jet black hair. She had been a bisexual teacher before her husband's death ten years ago, since which time she had became a straight lesbian.

"Men," she often said, "lack finesse in bed, yet they are demanding. I married because I wanted to have children. But it turned out that I can't conceive. So since my husband died I haven't so much as thought about sex with a man."

"Perhaps your husband wasn't a good lover?" I suggested.

"He wasn't the only man I had." she calmly said.

"I guess we are all made up different."

"Quite right, love. Some men love other men. Some persons even prefer animals."

She never commented on my seduction of boys, but I knew she knew. Through her I was able to keep abreast of the Douglases. And it was through her that I would enter the Douglases' home once more and execute the plan I had formulated to get even with Mrs Douglas and her big-cock husband.

Yes, I had a lovely plan for the Douglases. Often I would sit or lie back and allow my mind to picture how my revenge would unfold. First step would be to return to their bed like a prodigal

lover (when the time came I would ask Mrs Bailey to tell Mrs Douglas I wanted to visit her). I was sure they would accept me back as a lover, especially since I was to wait for another two or three years, when I would be wealthy and famous.

Then one night I would pay them a surprise visit with two well-paid girls and three equally well-paid and armed bisexual men. And a large German shepherd dog.

I didn't have to close my eyes to see the events which would follow.

In the face of our guns it would be all so easy. The Douglases would undress (if they had a live-in girl-servant-sexmate, we would tie her up and make her watch). We would take pictures of Mr Douglas in homosexual poses with one of the men. Then pictures of Mrs Douglas and the dog. (I was sure such pictures would ensure that the Douglases wouldn't seek legal action; plus I would have a firm alibi and proof that I had never met my escorts.)

After the pictures, Mr Douglas would be bound and buggered by my three male escorts and myself using a dildo; while the girls would be shaving Mrs Douglas' head. Then they would both be whipped.

But no need to be in a hurry, I mused, to execute my fine plan. The Douglases would never, I knew, leave Jamaica. I could, and would, wait for at least another two years, by which time I would be very wealthy and powerful.

And I would also be waiting for two or three years to get even with Carl – unless he came to pester me before then. In the meantime I would be concentrating on my business affairs and my one-year-old need for virgin boys.

Where seducing virgin boys was concerned I had a big plus in my favour. People's sexual bias. People never think of sex as soon as they see a woman with under-sixteen-year-old-boys, though sex, seduction and rape comes readily to mind as soon as they see a man and any age school girl. And while they will frown on a woman my age – mid-twenties – who seduces under-sixteen-year-old boys, they don't see such an act as being cruel or a crime in the

way they see a man in this twenties seducing under-sixteen-year-old girls as being a cruel and grave crime. Women like me they'll view as being a bit mad or very frigid. While the man who seduces young girls is seen as a beast.

Still, I guess I was very lucky that word of my love for boys didn't become public knowledge over the years I was constantly seducing virgin boys.

Chapter 28

As had been my plan, I began to use part of the upstairs as a night club in the second week of December, three weeks after my Schoolboys' Club had begun. The night club had its own entrance, via a narrow stairway built onto the side of the building, so the sections used as the Schoolboys' Club were sealed off from the night club customers.

The night club was really a disco with an adjoining room where pornographic movies were shown. No go-go dancing or striptease. I was the manager and had a bright, honest young man as my assistant.

The disco room had tables, a bar, a dance floor and was dimly lit, and there were flashing coloured lights aimed at the dance floor. The movie room was small and had comfortable love seats. The waitresses wore leotards with micro-mini skirts and high-heeled shoes. The waiters wore leotards with sports shoes.

The assistant manager soon fell in love with me and I took him as my lover. He was handsome with a small body, and was three years younger than me.

"Don't set your hopes too high," I told him after our first time on the divan in my office. "I lay any man or woman I think is worthy. So don't get too serious about your claim of love for me. Okay?"

"I don't care what you do as long as you don't pretend." His brown, oval face shone with sincerity in the soft light from the shaded floor lamps. "I love you."

I felt pity for him. "I guess I do love you as much as I will ever love any man." I sighed. "Perhaps I will decide to marry someday." That should give him hope, I thought, while reminding him he was my employee.

"If you do, I hope I will be the lucky man."

"I only know it would be a man as nice as you."

I was able to take two or three nights off each week knowing that the club was in competent and honest hands.

In January 1986 I met an angry looking young man at the door of the narrow stairway leading to the nightclub. It was about 8:30 p.m. on the Thursday night and we were both heading towards the disco. As soon as I came near him my in-built virgin detector system began to hum. No doubt about it, although he looked an angry twenty-five he was a virgin, and I had to have him.

"Hi," I said sweetly, "I am the owner and manger. Have you been here before?"

"Yes." He sounded sad. "Once."

"Like what we offer?" My pulse was racing excitedly, though I knew it was likely that he couldn't get it up for a nymph.

"Yea. It's okay."

"Perhaps you'd like to come to my office and give me a few suggestions which would improve our service?" I asked cosily. He was looking at me suspiciously. I added quickly, "We are new so I do welcome customers' advice."

"Sure," he said with a shrug.

I went up the stairs ahead of him, swinging my rear provocatively. I was wearing pink skin-tight pants and a white sweater. There were only a handful of customers in the disco room. Without delay I led my prey past my assistant manager, and through the door behind the bar that led to the rest of the upstairs area.

The skies had been overcast when I had left home, now there was a distant rumble of thunder when my prey and I entered my office. Was the thunder a sign from Mount Olympus?

I turned on the floor lamps, sat my prey in the purple love seat and asked, "Will you drink some wine with me?"

"Thanks." He sounded a bit nervous.

I took a bottle of very good wine and two glasses with ice from my small portable bar. I sat down beside him and poured the wine, then placed the bottle on the carpet.

"Now tell me what my disco-club lacks."

"The only thing I think you need is a live artiste now and again. You know, a singer and DJ now and again." Two large mouthfuls of my wine had settled his nerves somewhat and his dark brown face had lost its angry look.

My cunt was damp. I wanted him. "A good idea," I said huskily, moving closer to him. "But I might not try it out for a while yet."

He gulped the rest of his wine. I filled his glass again. "My name is Carlene. What's yours?"

"Dwight."

"Nice name." I now wanted him badly. "Kiss me, I want you." He was clearly surprised.

"Finish your wine and kiss me," I said, laying aside my glass. He gulped down his wine. I took his glass and attacked his mouth greedily. I led him to the divan and we undressed each other. His erect manhood glowed in the soft light, which was mellowed by the closed curtains at the windows.

He tried to get me onto my back. But that wouldn't do, I must claim all virginal sacrament in the divinely dominant female-on-top position. With some difficulty I was able to straddle him. I cried aloud in ecstasy when he entered me and next moment there was thunder and lightning – the gods and goddesses of Mount Olympus were pleased with this offering of adult virgin seed I was about to receive.

Shortly I felt his hot seed begin to spill forth inside my holy altar. My sacred ecstasy exploded with Olympian power. I screamed and slumped forward onto his broad hairy chest.

Seconds later, I felt stronger then ever before. "You are the best virgin I ever had." I wasn't looking at his face, but I felt his body stiffen. "Don't be ashamed," I added, "you did good. I am satisfied."

He was silent for a while before he said, embarrassed, "How did you guess?"

"I just have a natural talent for spotting virgin males. I really can't explain it. How old are you?"

"Twenty-four."

"You certainly weren't shy. How come you never had a woman before?" It was raining now and I was a bit chilly so I got up and began to put on my clothes. "You can stay here. I have to go look

out front, but first tell me why you didn't have any woman before now."

"I was trying to be a good christian," he said solemnly. "Then last month I found out that my father, who is a deacon, was seducing the young women. While my mother was having an affair with the priest." He sighed, "So I left the church and home."

"Do you think you and I sinned?"

He shrugged non-commitally. "It doesn't matter."

By now I was dressed. I sat down on the divan beside him. "I have for some time now been convinced that they made a grave mistake when they were translating the Bible. No type of sex between man and woman is sinful."

From then on I was on the look-out for adult virgins. Their seeds were stronger than the seeds of virgin boys. I found quite a few adult virgins but half of them had no use. Dead as a door nail.

The advent of AIDS into our island in 1987 made me cut back on the number of adult men I laid. And I insisted that those I did not know well use condoms. I travelled abroad for the first time in September that year, to Miami, and I bought a set of vibrators, including one that spurted a thick fluid when you pressed a button.

In November 1986 my brother's girl, Lorna, gave birth to a baby girl. It felt good to be an aunt and the sounds of a baby in my house brought out my maternal instincts. I seriously began to think of having a child of my own.

Who would I prefer to father my baby? Mr Black? My assistant club manager? The burly bar man? Or perhaps an unknown man?

I decided to wait until I was in my thirties before becoming a mother. And I would raise my child, or children, all alone as a single parent. Marry? Never, never!

Nineteen eighty-seven was a very prosperous year for me. My clubs made good profit, and I earned half a million dollars in profit from my marijuana business.

Then in 1988 Carl began to visit my night club occasionally, and, although he didn't approach me, my dream about him and me at sea began to recur at least twice each week. I became irritable, began to drink more and resumed smoking marijuana and cigarettes every day.

After five miserable months I decided that the only way I would return to normal was to get my revenge against Carl. I formulated a plan that depended on his being engaged to a girl. It was my intention to use my wealth, charms and body to steal his fiancé to be my live-in lover. I was sure I could do this, especially if I told the girl all I knew about him; and, of course, no man could give a girl as good a time in bed as I could.

In September I hired a detective who found out that Carl was now on staff at the University Hospital of the West Indies but was not seriously involved with a girl.

The detective's report was very disappointing. It seemed I would have to formulate a different plan. But it must be something that would hurt him badly, and he must know that it had been my handiwork. Perhaps I should, I thought, pay a gunman to kill him?

No, killing him would be a cruel act, especially since he wasn't bothering me now and had not bothered me for several years.

How about kidnapping him, I wondered, and castrating him, then releasing him? This would be right but he would surely bring down the law on my head. And whatever I did to him he must know it had been my work, otherwise my revenge would have been shallow – and I wasn't a shallow woman.

I knocked my brains but was unable to come up with a suitable plan. My original plan, I mused bitterly, would have been prefect for satisfying my ego. To have it known that a woman had taken away his betrothed would be devastating to any man, but more so for a 'playboy' like Carl.

Perhaps, I mused, he might soon become betrothed. Young doctors don't usually remain single for long, seeing that half of womankind dreams of marrying a doctor. Even one as slippery as Carl wouldn't be able to evade the ancient scheming of starry-eyed women.

177

I decided to stay my hand for a while to see if Carl would soon find himself betrothed. Then I would act.

So I turned my thoughts towards the Douglases and my plans for them. But before I could execute the first move towards the Douglases, Carl came at me, larger than life.

Chapter 29

Carl came at me on the night of the first Thursday in December 1988. The sun had been intense for weeks but this afternoon a modest shower of rain had fallen and since then a soothing breeze was blowing off the sea. At 8:00 p.m. I was in my office going over some figures and enjoying the cool breeze coming through the open windows along with the sounds of night traffic on Constant Spring Road, and music from the club.

There was a knock at the door,

"Come in," I called.

The door opened and a low hum of music from the club flowed around my assistant manager who was clearly disturbed. "There is a rather persistent man here asking to see you." This was one of the times when he was openly jealous of me, which wasn't often, so I always ignored the fact. Of course, if he became a pain in the ass I would have to get rid of him.

"What's his name?" I asked pleasantly.

"He refuses to..."

"It's only me," Carl said simply, joining my assistant in the doorway.

Dressed in brown – pants, jersey and beret – he looked like a prince, more handsome than ever, so handsome he took my breath away.

"Well? You know him?"

I was unable to speak and it took a lot of power to nod my head. All my hatred for Carl had been shoved aside by the beautiful picture he was to my eyes.

My assistant wheeled away.

Carl entered and closed the door, his eyes never leaving mine, moving with a seductively slow grace. My pulse was racing wildly and that strange warmth I felt in his presence now flooded my taut body.

Slowly he glanced around my moderately sized and comfort-

ably crowded office dominated by strong colours that now seemed alive in the bright lights.

Once his eyes left mine I was able to recall that I disliked him. But half of me wanted him sexually.

Then his eyes returned to me and he said, "I tried but couldn't bring myself to dislike or forget you. Now I know I stayed away too long. How about us now, my love?"

I stood up, anger and desire making it necessary for me to lean against, and hold onto, my desk. For several muddled seconds I couldn't find my voice and he was coming towards me.

"Please leave." It was intended to have been firm and contemptuous, but came out as a husky whisper. I tried again but did no better. "Please leave."

What he did was to come behind my desk and take me in his powerful arms and kiss me hard; one of his arms circled my sides pinning me to him and entrapping my arms at my sides; his other arm and hand held my head steady. For a few confusing seconds I struggled, but he was too strong for me, especially since I wasn't at my strongest. He forced me backwards against the golden drapes at the window behind my desk, my swivel chair was hard against my left leg. Then desire overcame my dislike, my knees went weak and I lost control of my dignity and senses, unable to stop my lips and the rest of my body from responding hungrily to his commanding kiss and embrace.

He released my hands and they flew upwards, then around his neck, my demented tongue feasting greedily on the sweetness of his mouth which was now soft against mine, my body washed by waves of pleasure.

I was now a mass of ecstasy, cemented by desire. Our lips parted. Both of us gasped breathlessly. Eyes locked. I was in need of his manhood. So I pushed him towards the divan. But he moved away from me and said unsteadily, eyes searching mine: "I don't want your body if you won't admit you are in love with me. Say the words, you know they are true and," (I was jolted back to reality) "I am hopelessly in love with you."

The words, 'I love you' almost shot out of my mouth.

"Carlene," he added softly, "I do love you."

My former ecstasy and desire had vanished, as if by magic. And I remembered that the bastard was using obeah to stir me sexually. So now he was taunting me with his power. "Get out, you devil!" I snarled – power from Olympus, didn't he know I wasn't a mere woman anymore.

"Damn it, Carlene, will you never forgive me!" he retorted. "What the hell must I do to make you realize I do love you, and make you admit your love for me." His face was flushed.

"Try killing yourself! You beast!" I was indignantly mad.

He glared at me. "When I kiss you, you melt. But as soon as I say the word 'love' you..."

"Get out! Go, you dog! I hate you!"

He sighed, turned and walked briskly from the room.

"The scheming bastard," I hissed angrily.

But a minute later I was curled up on the divan sobbing, and bewildered by a vague notion which was hovering on the outskirts of my consciousness. But why was I crying anyway?

I was now totally convinced Carl was using obeah to attract women. Now he was about to taunt me with his evil power. All he had said and done in my office had been for dramatic effect. Pure histrionics. He was a devil born amongst men, a royal tormentor.

It depressed me to know that a cruel man whom I despised could wield such great power over my sense and my body.

I thought of going to an obeah man, but that would've meant asking around for advice because I had never been to an obeah man or knew anyone who had been to one. So I decided to pay a gunman to kill Carl.

Killing the prick, I decided, would be my revenge and also free me from his evil clutches. Plus I would be doing other women a service. How many of my sisters had he trapped by obeah? Many, I was sure. Well, soon the devil wouldn't be able to hurt us any more.

My depression was made worse by the fact that Carl began to visit my night club regularly, alone or with friends. I thought of banning him from my premises, but knowing this would be bad for business I stayed in my office when he was around and told my assistant he wasn't to be allowed to approach my office. Whenever he came with a woman my hatred flared – Oh how, I thought, he must be abusing the poor woman with his obeah power.

It was degrading to have to hide in my office whenever he was around. But I was wise enough to know that it was best to go about planning his murder very carefully, without haste. The right plan had to be formulated, then the right gunman contacted. I had no intention of just pointing a gunman at him. Why? Point a gunman at him, gunman kills him and I pay the gunman, then a year or a few years later the murder is solved and the gunman sings my name. This I was determined wouldn't happen. No.

I would formulate an air-tight plan, complete with an alibi for the gunman, and then find an intelligent gunman – preferably a policeman – to do the job.

Time, and rational thinking. By the end of 1989 I should be able to rid the earth of its most low-down prick.

I had to increase my drinking and smoking in order to be able to sleep. But although the recurring dream about Carl and me at sea was now invading my sleep several times each week I was able to ignore it, knowing I would soon have him murdered. Peace.

The year 1989 saw a great increase in my sexual needs – boys, girls, men, women. I became almost insatiable.

In June 1989 I was well on my way to formulating the perfect plan for Carl's murder when tragedy struck on a Monday night.

Chapter 30

It had been an unusually slow night at the club, even for a Monday night. Both the disco and video rooms were almost empty when I left the club in my assistant's hands at 1:00 a.m. I had had two boys and a girl in the afternoon and two men in the night, so I was as high as I possibly could be when the younger of my two brothers and I went down the narrow stairway into the night (my younger brother had come to live and work with me in October 1988; and this night was my other brother's night off from his job as bouncer). Outside it was cool and the clear, moonless sky was thick with stars. I wasn't drunk – I always made sure I wasn't whenever I had to drive.

Ten minutes later, I was speeding my new B.M.W. up the well-lit and almost empty Hope Road – half of my mind was devising my plan to kill Carl – when an old Mercedes Benz, which was speeding down the road, swerved out of control and came rushing towards me.

I swung my wheel hard left. But I was too late. The Benz rammed straight into me (and you know how tough the 1960s Benz are!). There was an ear-splitting bang of metal and I felt as if I was spinning at lightning speed. Then I lost consciousness.

Miraculously my brother escaped with only a few minor cuts. The driver of the Benz wasn't seriously injured but he had fainted after looking at my twisted, bleeding body, sure I was dead. The police and an ambulance were quickly on the scene but it took a while to get my body from behind the steering wheel.

It seemed that the driver of the Benz had been drunk and had fallen asleep at the wheel.

Forty-four hours later I awoke in a small, well-lit room at a private hospital. For several seconds everything whirled and was blurred. Was I dead?

Then my vision cleared a bit and I saw that I was in a flower-bedecked room, lying in a small hospital bed and strung up to var-

ious intravenous solutions and blood. Next I saw a vague outline of a nurse enter the room. I wanted to call but my voice failed and sleep overcame me.

When I next awoke, it was midday, and there were two doctors and a nurse at my bedside. After several blurry seconds my vision cleared and I became aware of various aches and numbness all over my body. I felt complete lifeless, but my mind was clear.

"Hello," one doctor said. "Do you see me clearly." He was tall, slim, middle-aged and his brown face was cheerful.

I nodded, then mumbled, "Yes." My mouth tasted awful.

"Fine. I am Dr Grant. You'll be alright soon. You seem to be a very brave girl so I am going to give you the bad news now."

I stiffened.

"Nothing fatal," Dr Grant said soothingly. His young colleague looked as solemn as an undertaker. "In addition," Dr Grant said, "to a broken arm, several fractured ribs and some bad cuts, we had to remove your right leg."

Do they give jokes in hospitals? Still I gaped and looked on. The sheets did seem a bit flat where my right foot should be. But my right leg and foot were there, didn't I just wiggle my right toes?

Next moment the solemn young female doctor shattered my world by lifting the sheet so I could see the bandaged stump of my right thigh. I gasped and tried to sit up, but the cruel female doctor and the sympathetic nurse held me back against the spotlessly white pillow.

Dr Grant launched into a morale boosting speech, but I only half-heard him. The loss of a leg was a very great blow. But I didn't think of dying; through my mind was flashing the things I wouldn't be able to do again – run, dance, jump and straddle virgin boys.

Dr Grant's speech ended.

"Any special requests?" the lady doctor asked grimly.

"No." I glared at her.

So I was now a one-legged woman. My plan was to buy a home on the sea coast, leave my clubs to Mr Black and my employ-

ees and live out the rest of my life in quiet seclusion. No more smuggling. No sex, neither boys, girls, man nor woman.

Was my fate as a one-legged woman, I wondered, the work of God, payment for a loose life? Punishment for sex with other women and my silly pretence that bedding virgin boys was an Olympian act? And wanting to kill Carl?

I couldn't say why, but for the first time in my life I knew that the God of Moses, Isaiah, Peter, James and John was real. It was just a feeling I got deep in my soul, especially when the various evangelists were allowed to visit my room.

My thoughts often went to Carl, causing me a strange and empty sadness. I no longer wanted revenge against him and the Douglases. What was the use of wanting revenge when I would soon be a lonely, nun-like woman? The dream about Carl and me at sea ceased and in its place came confusing dreams I couldn't recall upon awakening but always had a vague feeling each had begun with Carl and me getting married.

My brothers and their girlfriends, Mr Black, Momma, Daddy and a steady flow of my employees visited me regularly, and did a lot to lift my spirits. But what helped the most was that after two weeks matron and the doctors had to break the rules and allow my niece, who was now two and a half years old, to visit me. Since my accident she had been crying for me and had all but stopped eating, and finally her doctor phoned and asked my doctors to overlook her age and allow her to visit me – hospital rules said children under twelve years weren't allowed to visit the sick in their rooms, and I was confined to bed.

I was alarmed to see how thin she looked when her father brought her to my room.

"Auntie Carlie," she sobbed, "they didn't want me to come see you, and I dream you was dead." She was sitting on a chair close by my bed, clutching my hand, her tearful baby-face showing childish relief that I was really alive.

Love of the purest kind flooded me. "My little love, the hos-

pital has a rule that little children mustn't enter the room because they might get sick. Now I want you to promise me you'll begin to eat a lot as soon as you go home. Promise?"

She nodded. Her father had dried her tears.

My spotless room was always filled with flowers, so I was able to cope with the dullness of the furniture and the dreary and empty pale-yellow walls; I was using my own brightly coloured bed linen. And the nurses were a kind and cheerful lot.

After a week of thought I had concluded that the loss of my leg wasn't a divine act. Didn't some of the kindest and most upright people die young or become disabled, while murderers and other evil persons lived to a ripe old age without changing from their evil ways? Weren't thousands born disabled? So why would God have taken one of my legs because of sins which weren't that great?

True, I mused, I had been intent on killing Carl, but surely God wasn't on the side of obeah workers such as Carl. Vengeance is mine, saith the Lord, but he wouldn't take away a leg because one intended to kill someone like Carl.

On my eighteenth day in the hospital, Carl came with a single rose. Knocked the wind out of my sails and brought me, or rather, steered me into a new world.

Chapter 31

When he entered the room I began to tremble slightly. I was propped up in bed reading a magazine. He was wearing brown pants and a doctor's jacket, clearly he was either on his way to or from the University Hospital.

"Hello, Carlene," he said forcing a smile as he came towards me slowly, our eyes locked, holding the red rose before him like a priceless treasure.

I felt guilty and ashamed, because it was clear even to my eyes that he did care about me. "Hello, Carl," I responded shakily.

He took one of my hands, causing excitement to shock my weary body with energetic ecstasy. "I brought this single red rose as a sign of my undying love." He stuck the rose in my hair. "I need you Carlene, and I am ordering you to face up to our love and marry me."

It was now clear to me that what I had always felt with Carl was the magnetism of true love. "What use will a one-legged woman be to you?" I blurted, our eyes locked. "Especially one who was planning to kill you."

He frowned in bewilderment.

"I was convinced," I added wistfully and penitently, "that the reason your presence always excited me was because you were using obeah oil," (he was losing his bewildered frown) "to attract me." I was searching his face. "You see, I was sure I hated you." I looked away.

"My love," he said soothingly, "none of that matters. I shouldn't have forced you to have sex with me when you were working with my mother." He caressed my hair.

I gazed into his eyes. "I now know I do love you. But what will your parents say if you marry me?"

"What they think and say won't matter to me. I need you. As my wife."

"Oh, Carl..."

"Carl and Carlene."

LaVergne, TN USA
09 September 2009
157240LV00001B/20/A